Praise for W. Bruce Cameron, author of the
beloved #1 *New York Times* and *USA Today*
bestselling novel *A Dog's Purpose*

"A book about dog lovers by an author who understands the
canine soul."
—*Kirkus Reviews* on *The Dogs of Christmas*

"Another winning tale of an extraordinary human-canine
companionship full of tug-at-the-heartstrings adventure."
—*Booklist* on *A Dog's Way Home*

"I loved the book and I could not put it down."
—Temple Grandin, *New York Times* bestselling
author of *Animals in Translation,*
on *A Dog's Purpose*

"Readers will devour this wonderful story and cry from beginning to end. Sweet and heartfelt, Cameron likely has
another bestseller on his hands."
—*Publishers Weekly* (starred review)
on *A Dog's Journey*

BY W. BRUCE CAMERON

A Dog's Purpose
Emory's Gift
A Dog's Journey
The Dogs of Christmas
The Dog Master
A Dog's Way Home

REPO MADNESS SERIES

The Midnight Plan of the Repo Man
Repo Madness

FOR YOUNGER READERS

Ellie's Story: A Dog's Purpose Puppy Tale
Bailey's Story: A Dog's Purpose Puppy Tale
Molly's Story: A Dog's Purpose Puppy Tale
Max's Story: A Dog's Purpose Puppy Tale

8 Simple Rules for Dating My Teenage Daughter
How to Remodel a Man
8 Simple Rules for Marrying My Daughter

THE DOGS
OF CHRISTMAS

W. BRUCE CAMERON

A TOM DOHERTY ASSOCIATES BOOK

NEW YORK

THE DOGS OF CHRISTMAS

Copyright © 2013 by W. Bruce Cameron

"About Eighteen Months Later" copyright © 2018 by W. Bruce Cameron

A Forge Book
Published by Tom Doherty Associates
175 Fifth Avenue
New York, NY 10010

www.tor-forge.com

Forge® is a registered trademark of Macmillan Publishing Group, LLC.

The Library of Congress has cataloged the hardcover edition as follows:

Cameron, W. Bruce.
    The dogs of Christmas / W. Bruce Cameron.—1st ed.
     p. cm.
    "A Tom Doherty Associates book."
    ISBN 978-0-7653-3055-0 (hardcover)
    ISBN 978-1-4299-9287-9 (ebook)
    1. Dogs—Fiction. 2. Dogs—Breeding—Fiction. 3. Puppies—
Fiction. 4. Human-animal relationships—Fiction. 5. Christmas stories.
I. Title.
PS3603.A4535D66 2013
813'.6—dc23

                                      2013018448

ISBN 978-1-250-20353-3 (trade paperback)

Our books may be purchased in bulk for promotional, educational, or business use. Please contact your local bookseller or the Macmillan Corporate and Premium Sales Department at 1-800-221-7945, extension 5442, or by email at MacmillanSpecialMarkets@macmillan.com.

First Edition: October 2013
First Trade Paperback Edition: October 2018

Printed in the United States of America

0 9 8 7 6 5 4

To the people all over the world who have
opened their hearts and their homes
to orphaned animals

THE DOGS
OF CHRISTMAS

ONE

The phone rang.

Josh looked over at it, not sure if he'd heard correctly. A muscular contraction twitched its way up his spine, something like a false start toward answering it. The leather chair he was sitting in made a whispering noise as he shifted. He unconsciously lowered his book, as if that would help him see who was calling, somehow.

The date was October first. Nobody's birthday, no holiday—no reason for anyone to be calling.

It rang again.

His eyes drifted over to Amanda's picture on the table next to him, and that's why he stood up. In all probability it was a wrong number or, worse, a solicitation to buy something or insure something or do something. But remembering what it was like to hear her voice on the line irresistibly compelled him to cross the room and reach for the phone before it rolled to voice mail—though he knew, of course, that it could not be Amanda.

He didn't recognize the number in his caller ID. "Hello?"

"Michael! Dude, you don't answer your cell phone? I left you like five messages."

Josh was frowning, trying to place the voice squawking in his ear.

"I need your help, buddy. I have a major situation," the caller continued.

"Sorry, who is this?"

"It's Ryan. Your neighbor? Come on, Michael, you remember me."

"My name's not Michael," was all Josh could think to say. Ryan? Who the heck was Ryan? "It's Josh Michaels."

"Right, well, that just proves how stressed I am. Josh. Remember me? Brews at the Little Bear?"

The Little Bear was an old-west-style saloon that had been in the mountain town of Evergreen virtually since there had been an Evergreen. The place was always crowded— Josh sometimes went there because being packed in with so many people gave him the illusion that he was popular.

Brews at the Little Bear. Oh. Right. Josh briefly closed his eyes. Yes. *Ryan.* A shared conversation built on the misconception that their circumstances were similar. *You're lucky,* Ryan had said. *I got thrown out, had to find my own place even though I was unemployed and completely broke. Your deal, I know it sounds harsh, but in the end you've got a place to live.*

Lucky? That he'd lost Amanda?

Not lucky. Amanda was gone but still here, her scent still imagined on the air, her presence just outside the periphery of Josh's vision, the bed heavy in the dark with a sleeping form that was really only shadow and memory. It took a special kind of stupid to call that lucky.

And Ryan, Josh now recalled, was precisely that stupid. The man had listened to Josh's tale of loss with the impatient expression of a debater waiting for his time at the microphone, plunging into a rant the moment Josh finished speaking. Ryan hated his old girlfriend. Hunched over a beer and making gathering motions as if enlisting Josh as an accomplice, Ryan spoke in hot, resentful terms about his breakup, all but suggesting he was due some sort of justice and, if not that, revenge. What was her name? Well, that didn't matter. Josh just remembered feeling more and more distant from Ryan, watching him from across the table, then as if from across the room, and then as if from far, far away.

Had he really given this person his phone number?

"You said to call if I needed any help with anything," Ryan reminded Josh, answering the unspoken question.

"Right, you said you tried to light a fire in your woodstove and the house filled with smoke." The last thing anyone would want up here at 8,500 feet, living among lodgepole pines desiccated by Japanese beetles, was for some idiot to burn his cabin down. As Josh recalled, his offer of assistance had been limited to ensuring Ryan didn't set fire to the entire mountainside.

"Well, this is like that times a thousand. My brother—you're not going to believe this—got arrested. In *France*." Ryan proclaimed this last word with a triumphant emphasis.

Josh waited a moment so that Ryan could explain what this had to do with him. "So . . . ," he finally prodded.

"So I need your help, bro. I've got Serena's dog here. Someone needs to watch it."

That was the ex-girlfriend's name. Serena. "Well, no, I can't," Josh replied.

"Dude, I have got to go to Europe! They won't let you take dogs there and anyway it's not even my dog and I have to leave right away on a flight in like four hours. Okay? Can you hear how I'm really stressed here? Loose and I are coming over, I'll explain it then."

"Loose?"

"Its name's Loose, what can I tell you."

Josh took in a deep breath, but the firm and unequivocal statement he intended to deliver was snuffed out by the dead tone that blanketed the line once Ryan clicked off.

Josh went to his window, a floor-to-ceiling expanse of paned glass next to the front door from which he could see his front deck and the yard and driveway beyond. The air was dry and clear this October afternoon, sun streaming down through the trees as if poured from a bucket. Amanda loved to hike on a day like this, a Saturday. They'd find a mountain trail and she'd be tireless, always ready to keep going. Ironically, she'd always wanted a dog, but Josh, picturing all the extra work that would go into taking care of a pet, said no. He saw himself as too busy for a dog.

If they'd gotten one, though, then Josh would have had a friend to help him mourn her. Wasn't that the thing about dogs, that they stood by you no matter what? That was Josh's impression, anyway.

Though their homes on the sparsely populated hillside were less than a hundred yards apart, Ryan drove over. He was apparently one of those people who kept his vehicle in full-time four-wheel drive because he lived in the mountains and thought that's what you needed to do. Josh watched all four of the oversized tires bite the dirt as the SUV bounded up the switchback. It came to a grinding halt, rocking, and Ryan stepped out of the vehicle.

He was dressed the way Josh would be for air travel, wearing khaki pants, a sweater, and a light jacket. He gave a slight wave at Josh through the window, and Josh crossed to his front door, deciding to prevent Ryan and his dog Loose from their intended trespass. He stepped out on the deck, his boots ringing on the boards.

"Hey, Josh," Ryan called as if they were the best of buddies.

Immediately after losing Amanda, Josh had let his hair and beard grow, just like Ryan's—the whiskers not bushy, exactly, but sculpted into a permanent ten-days' growth, the hair brushing his collar. Then during a teleconference Josh noticed his clients eyeing him and realized that he was pushing people toward a conclusion they were already willing to embrace, that he was some sort of lone nut living in a cabin on a mountain, coding applications in the day and then at night, what, running with the wolves? Building bombs out of wood pieces? Josh went back to the clean-shaven look, his dark hair short, and now Ryan's wooly appearance, stringy blond hair down past his ears, reinforced the wisdom of Josh's decision. Ryan looked as if he'd joined a cult that was against grooming.

"I appreciate this big time, buddy," Ryan said gratefully.

"I can't do it, Ryan. I've never even had a dog before. I don't know the first thing about taking care of them."

Ryan raised his hands to his head and winced as if he were having a migraine. "Can I just explain? This is serious. Do you even know what the laws are like in Europe? It's like, Canada times a thousand. I have to hire a lawyer who speaks like both French and English, how am I going to do that? My brother's arrested and it's just totally messed up."

Josh sifted through all of this carefully, looking for the part that explained why he should provide care for Ryan's ex-girlfriend's dog. He couldn't find it. "Can't she just take him back?"

A canine face, brown and black, rose up in the back of the SUV, looking out the window at the two men. A pink tongue peeped into view.

"Who, Serena? She's traveling. And anyway she dumped the dog like she did me, that's who she is, man, I told you. Look, just . . . it's just for a few days. I'll call you as soon as I'm settled in France, and I'll make arrangements from there to have someone pick him up, okay? But I have to go *now*."

Josh steeled himself. "Look, this isn't my problem, Ryan. I'm sorry about your brother. But I can't take a *dog*. It's impossible."

"Well, then, what am I going to do?" Ryan asked, lifting arms out to his sides and then dropping them flat on his hips. "There's supposed to be a storm coming. I just let the dog go and it'll freeze. There. The dog dies."

"You're being ridiculous."

"I'm leaving for Europe!" Ryan shouted in frustration. "Are you going to help me out here, or not?"

No. That's what Josh was going to say. *No, I will not help you out. Get off my property.* But he glanced involuntarily at the dog before he spoke, and what he saw in those eyes made him hesitate. Suddenly, he took everything in from Loose's perspective. Its owner gone, something that defied canine explanation. Living with Ryan, a man who felt that a flight to France, a place in Europe, preempted all other concerns, human and otherwise. Ryan probably would just abandon the poor animal, just as he was threatening. Loose would be bewildered and alone. The dog probably *would* die.

"I . . . ," Josh faltered helplessly.

Ryan saw something in Josh's expression and seized it.

"Thanks, man, I owe you." Ryan walked around to the back of his SUV. "I promise as soon as I get things figured out, I'll call you. This is for like two or three days, max. I have the food right here."

Ryan lifted the gate and, with a moment's hesitation, a large dog, marked like a shepherd but with something else mixed in, leaped heavily to the ground. It shook, raised its head to Ryan for a touch that wasn't forthcoming, and then trotted up to Josh, its head lowered and its tail beating the ground submissively.

Josh's mouth was open in shock at the sight of the big dog. He put his hand down and was nuzzled with a wet nose, but his surprise choked off anything he might say.

"And here's a bowl, too," Ryan announced, lugging a brightly colored bag of food up onto the deck and setting down a metal bowl that clanged when it struck the wood.

"You said this was a male," Josh objected. "Named Loose."

"Yeah." Ryan squinted at him while Josh ran his index finger along the name embroidered on the dog's collar.

"This says *Lucy*. Not Loose. Lucy."

Ryan shrugged. "Serena always called him Loose, what do I know?"

"Not him, Ryan. It's not him. It's her. Lucy. The female dog," Josh corrected sharply.

"Fine." Ryan spread his hands in a *what's the difference* gesture.

"Not fine. It's not just that she's female. She's obviously pregnant, can't you see? Lucy is a *pregnant* female dog."

TWO

"Are you sure?" Ryan asked after a moment. His eyes slid away guiltily.

Josh glanced down at the dog, who sat, her ears erect and her brown eyes clear. "Am I sure? *Look* at her! Look at her teats. Did you think she was just fat?"

"Okay, well, but in my defense I knew that if I told you Loose was pregnant you wouldn't take her. And you said yourself you're not some kind of dog expert," Ryan reasoned.

"That's your *defense*?" Josh sputtered.

Ryan turned around and started walking away. The dog watched him uncertainly, coming to her feet but not moving from Josh's side.

"Where are you going?"

"I don't have time!" Ryan snapped, shutting his tailgate with a bang. "I have to go."

"Yes, I know, you have to go to France. I'm sorry about your brother. But you're going to have to make some other arrangements. I can't have a pregnant dog."

"Well, but first you said you couldn't have a dog at all, and you changed your mind on that."

Josh watched in disbelief as Ryan opened his car door.

"Wait, what are you doing?" Josh demanded. "We're not done. You can't just leave. Hey!"

When Ryan shut his door, Josh realized that just leaving was exactly what Ryan intended. Josh strode briskly across his yard, prepared to knock on the driver's side window and, if necessary, fling open the door. He could see himself doing it, maybe even grabbing Ryan and pulling the man to the ground. You don't up and drive away in the middle of a conversation, especially when the conversation is *you can't leave your dog here.*

The dog followed on Josh's heels, yawning anxiously. Ryan started the vehicle and, astoundingly, engaged his transmission, his four chunky tires spitting dirt back at Josh, who dashed after it. "Stop! You can't do this!" he shouted.

Naturally the SUV pulled away, and Josh, defeated, slowed and then stopped. "Just great," he muttered as the vehicle slid around the switchback and dropped down the hill out of sight. His own keys were on the kitchen table—he could dash in, grab the dog, and take off in hot pursuit. But then what? With that kind of head start, Josh stood little chance of even seeing Ryan on the road, so he'd have to drive all the way out to the airport. Denver International Airport was huge and Josh had no idea which airline Ryan was taking. And would the authorities really prevent the man from flying to France on the basis of an abandoned dog?

Josh warily regarded Lucy, who had stopped following when Josh elected to chase after the vehicle—maybe she'd tried it a few times before on other cars and had come to conclude there was no profit in it. She was sitting at the top of the driveway, watching him, perhaps waiting for an explanation. Probably sitting was her main activity, now—her belly was hugely swollen with the pups inside her, the teats pronounced, her body heavy. She looked nine-months' pregnant—or however many months it took a dog. She watched him alertly as he crunched back up the driveway.

"So here's what we're going to do," Josh decided. The dog raised her ears a little at this, apparently glad there was a plan. "We'll call somebody. The vet, I mean. Okay? There's no way I can take care of you; I don't know the first thing about delivering puppies."

Lucy regarded him with her warm dark eyes. The trust in them was almost unbearable to behold, given that Josh had just told her he was essentially going to dump her off on someone else. That seemed to have been happening to Lucy a lot lately. Where was the ex-girlfriend, anyway? What sort of person leaves a pregnant dog with someone like Ryan?

Josh sighed and looked around his property. When Josh's father first built the house, the skinny lodgepole pines blanketing the hillside had been beaten back about two dozen yards, Josh's mother optimistically planting city grass and flowers. Over time, though, the foreign foliage had gasped and died in the thin, dry air, and now coarse, native ground cover, brown except in June, lay matted at his feet. A stand of aspen trees had steadily advanced out of the woods like eighteenth-century soldiers, and they always went to color early: already some of the leaves were full gold, sunlight bouncing off them in flaring explosions of yellow. Painted against the dark evergreens, it was almost too bright to look at. It made him restless, all this beautiful scenery, as if he'd been wasting his day buried in a book when he should have been out on the trails, drinking in the afternoon. But he wouldn't be going anywhere, now—Lucy didn't look in any shape to be taking a hike.

"Are you okay?" Josh tentatively patted her head and she thumped her tail, her eyes closing a little. That was pretty much the sum total of his knowledge of dog behavior, right there—you petted them and they wagged their tails. "Do you need to lie down? Are you hungry? Let's go inside. You're housebroken, right? Does being pregnant affect that?"

This was insane. He couldn't take care of a *dog*.

When he walked in his front door, Lucy hesitated on the threshold until he slapped his thigh, and then she entered cautiously, nose down.

It was a hardwood floor—he couldn't ask a pregnant animal to lie down on that. He dashed into his bedroom and, after only a moment's hesitation, grabbed what he had always thought of as Amanda's pillow. "Here," he offered, setting it down on a rug. Lucy sniffed it. "Want a blanket?" In the closet there was a quilt. Josh pulled this down and sort of fluffed it under the pillow. "There."

Lucy regarded him blankly. "Oh! Let me move it into the sunshine for you," Josh exclaimed. He rearranged the bed in a square of sun cast from the front window. This time, when he patted it, Lucy waddled over to him and lay down on the soft assembly with a groan.

"Wow, you're really big. I mean, not fat. Well, you're a little fat. But mostly pregnant—you're really, really pregnant. I guess you know that."

Lucy gave him a disdainful glance and Josh realized he was babbling a little, and that he was pretty close to a flat-out panic. It wasn't even two in the afternoon—less than half an hour ago he'd been curled up with a novel and now he had this poor pregnant dog to take care of and all he could think to do was insult her about her weight. What was he going to do?

"Could I speak to the vet?" Josh asked when the receptionist answered his call. "I just had a neighbor drop off his dog and leave for France, and the dog is pretty pregnant, and I need to make sure I'm doing the right thing and everything. Also, you know, to bring her in so she can have her puppies."

"You want to bring her in? Is she in labor now?" the woman on the other side of the phone asked.

"I don't know. I mean, how would I know, do they . . . what do they do? Do they bark?"

She laughed. "No, not normally. Is she pacing, panting, crying, or vomiting?"

"No." *But I nearly am.*

"Any discharge of fluids?"

"I don't see any." *Yuck.*

She asked him to hold and after several minutes a man picked up the phone and introduced himself as Dr. Becker. Josh told him the story and explained what he needed.

"Actually, dog birth usually happens in the home. You'd

pretty much only need to bring her in if there were complications," Dr. Becker informed him.

"Sure, yeah, but I don't, I mean, I've never even had a dog before. My dad was allergic to them growing up."

"Are you allergic?"

"No." Josh felt defensive. "It's just that when you've never had a dog, you don't think to get one."

"Do you think you could take Lucy's temperature?"

"I don't know. I mean, how? Won't she just bite it?"

Dr. Becker laughed. "Well, no, you need to be thinking of this from the other end," he explained, saying Josh could use a little margarine to lubricate the thermometer. Josh swallowed and Lucy raised her head to look at him as if reading his mind. What kind of way was *that* to introduce yourself to a dog? *Hey, you're fat. Turn around, I've got something for you.*

"I'll have to buy a thermometer," Josh speculated. "I don't have one in the house."

"That's fine. If the temperature drops below a hundred degrees, she should deliver within twenty-four hours."

Deliver. Josh shook his head. "I think maybe I should just bring her in, Dr. Becker. I'm sorry, but I just don't think I'm going to be any good at this."

"Let's see. We're closing up soon, and we're not open Sundays. Why don't you bring her in Monday morning for an examination?"

"Uh, sure. I have a teleconference in the morning, but I could be there by noon."

"That's fine. But Josh?"

"Yeah?"

"I want you to understand that we won't be boarding your dog unless there are medical complications requiring it. We clear?"

"But . . ."

"I'll examine Lucy and we can talk more about the birthing experience, but you need to take responsibility for your dog."

"Okay," Josh acquiesced weakly. After he hung up, he turned away from the phone. "But it's not my dog," he said aloud.

Lucy watched him as he carried the sack of dog food into the kitchen. He poured some of it into the metal bowl and she eased to her feet and padded over to it, putting her nose into her dinner. Josh watched as she picked out a mouthful of the little unappetizing pellets, dropped them on the floor, and then ate them one by one from there.

"Is that good, Lucy? Good dinner? Good dog dinner?" He doubted it—when he sniffed the open bag he didn't smell anything suggestive of food.

She ate a little, then drank some water he set out for her, and then sat and looked at him.

"What? Do you need something? Are you okay? You're not having contractions, are you?" Josh crouched down and peered into her eyes. "You're going to be fine."

Josh picked up Ryan's phone number off his caller ID and dialed. It rolled straight to voice mail. "Hello, Ryan, this is Josh, here. You're probably still in the air. When you land, please call me, okay? I've talked to the vet, and I'm taking

Lucy there Monday. I'll obviously expect that you'll pay me back for the appointment. And let me know, please, when you've made permanent arrangements as we agreed. Okay, then. Have a safe flight."

Josh was wincing as he hung up. Have a safe flight? *Look here,* he should have said, *you take care of this situation or I'll beat the crap out of you.*

Josh had never beaten the crap out of anybody, but there was no way Ryan would know that.

Monday afternoon seemed a long way off from the perspective of this Saturday afternoon. What was he going to do until then?

Even though Lucy was probably days, or even weeks, from delivering, Josh decided to move her bedding into his bedroom so he could monitor her condition during the night. He waited until she was up off the pillow and sniffing around in the kitchen so it wouldn't inconvenience her. "You'll be fine," he kept repeating, hoping that was true. She looked so *sad.* Was she scared? Homesick? Josh would be feeling both. "Poor dog," he soothed. "I'm sorry, Lucy."

That night, whenever she moved he was instantly awake, rolling over to look at her. "You okay?"

Lucy got tired of wagging her tail each time he asked this and soon would just sigh in reply.

Sunday, Lucy didn't really do much—she mostly just lay on her pillow in the living room. Josh thawed some ground bison in the microwave and gave it to her so she wouldn't have a diet of nothing but the cheap pellets. He found a tennis ball and put it next to her, but she didn't seem to want to play with it. He moved her water bowl next to her and covered her with a small blanket. He rubbed her back, recalling that he'd heard somewhere that this was something that women liked when they were pregnant.

He felt desperately inadequate. What else should he do? His Internet search turned up frustratingly little about how to make a pregnant dog feel better after she's been dumped off by someone headed to France. It had more to say about making pregnant *women* feel better, but it didn't seem transferable. Like, foot rubs? Can you do a foot rub on a dog's paw?

He hated leaving her alone late Sunday afternoon, but he couldn't see the sense in taking her to the grocery store with him. Lucy was watching him from the big window as he drove off in his pickup truck, and the wounded expression he imagined he saw nearly broke his heart. *I am not abandoning you. I am not Ryan. I am not Serena.* In town he bought a thermometer and some high-quality dog food and a rawhide bone and a pull toy with a squeaker in it. He also bought a Frisbee and chicken strips and a rope dog toy and a monkey dog toy and a tiger dog toy.

Lucy was there to greet him, wagging, when he opened the door, his packages crinkling. He sat on the floor with her and presented her with each toy in turn, and she wagged while sniffing each one and gave the rawhide bone a bit of a chewing, but Josh felt pretty sure she was just humoring him. Mostly she seemed to want to just concentrate on being pregnant.

He was already in bed when he remembered the thermometer, still in the package on the kitchen counter. "We'll do it in the morning," he told Lucy. "I don't think you'll mind waiting." Josh sure wouldn't, anyway.

Her bed was where he'd placed it the night before. At around four in the morning, Josh woke up with a frown, wondering what had disturbed his sleep. He rolled over on an elbow to check on the dog.

His eyes widened. Lucy was not in her bed. She was gone.

THREE

Lucy?" Josh sat up, cocking his head. The floor was cool beneath his feet as he padded into the living room. Moonlight washed in through the windows, painting the colors out of the house with its stark white. Lucy was in the kitchen, standing in front of the oven, panting and trembling a little. "Hey, girl," Josh whispered, alarmed. "You okay?"

Lucy licked her lips. She brushed past him, went into the living room, circled around on the rug, and lay down. A second later she was up again, pacing in front of the door.

"Do you need to go out?" Josh asked. He went to the door and pulled it open and Lucy dashed out into the yard. She stopped, squatting, and forcefully ejected a wet pile that was black in the moonlight.

"I guess the ground buffalo was a bad idea, huh?" Josh observed, relieved that's all it was. "Probably not so smart to change your diet all at once, either. Did it make you sick to your stomach, Lucy?"

She seemed a lot better when she came back to the house. "Okay, good dog. I'm sorry about that."

Lucy settled down on her bed next to his and eased back into sleep, but when the alarm woke him up at 7:30 A.M. she wasn't there. Josh found her in the back bedroom, of all places, lying in the small space between the bed and the wall. "What are you doing, Lucy?" he asked. She wagged and followed him into the kitchen, but when he set out a mix of her cardboard pellets and the good stuff, called Nature's Variety, she didn't do anything more than sniff at it and then gaze at him with a mournful expression.

"Tummy still upset? I'm so, so sorry," Josh apologized. Less than forty-eight hours with a dog and he'd almost poisoned it with raw buffalo. "You go to the vet after my meeting, Lucy. They know how to take care of you there. I don't. Trust me, your life's going to be a lot easier." He avoided her gaze as he said this, though, feeling guilty about it. It was true, though, right? Even if being taken to yet another place to stay might be disorienting, it would all be for the best once she went into labor.

His own breakfast was a microwave muffin and a cup of coffee. Josh showered and dove into his e-mail and then tinkered with the chart he planned to upload during his client conference, distracted and not paying attention to Lucy, who went back to her bed, or back down the hallway where the bedrooms were, anyway. It wasn't until he was pouring himself another cup of coffee that Josh glanced at the thermometer and remembered, with a guilty start, that he had an unpleasant obligation to take care of. "Oh, Lucy," he muttered to himself.

The news just keeps getting worse.

He let the dog out in case she needed to make another deposit in the yard, thinking that he didn't want to be standing behind her with a thermometer when *that* happened.

Lucy just trotted out into the yard and stood looking at him, so he waved at her and she came back in, giving him a *what was the point of that?* look.

Josh caught sight of his face in a mirror as he was lubricating the thermometer with margarine. His eyes were slits, his mouth hanging open in slack horror. He forced himself to look normal. "Here we go, Lucy," he grated. "We got to do this."

Taking her temperature was every bit as enjoyable as he thought it would be. What he saw, though, made his blood freeze.

Ninety-seven and a half. Her temperature was ninety-seven degrees! And below a hundred meant that within twenty-four hours . . .

Oh, come on. This could *not* be happening. Wasn't it just Saturday that his life was completely normal, or at least as normal as it had been since losing Amanda? Now he was going to have puppies!

"Ryan," Josh sternly lectured his neighbor's voice mail, his heart pounding, "you need to call me back. Lucy's temperature is below a hundred, which means she's going to be in labor before we know it. I need you to get on this right now. I'll remind you that animal abandonment is a crime." *Probably not extraditable from France, though.* "I'll take her to the vet, but whoever it is who is going to take care of the dog needs to get involved quickly, and needs to be ready for puppies by sometime tomorrow. Got that? Call me!"

Lucy went back to the bedroom, probably vowing never to speak to him again after the whole thermometer incident.

His conference call was coming up; he had to get ready. He put on a clean shirt and conscientiously logged into the conference before anyone else. He adjusted his camera, cleared his throat, and then one by one people popped into the virtual room on the screen.

The project manager was Gordon Blascoe. He was a bald man with glasses who was known for terse e-mails that everyone called Blascoe's Blurts.

"I'm seeing that the project timeline has gotten extended into the second quarter again," Blascoe complained, launching right into discussion without greeting or preamble. "Since the deadline is February fifteenth I don't get how this happened."

"It's the new tasks," someone chimed in. "Because, you know, adding dependencies—things that have to be done before the tasks themselves can be considered done—extends the timeline."

Blascoe never seemed to understand how his project management software worked, how adding tasks automatically rippled through the project, pushing everything out. They had conversations like this one about once every two weeks. Josh wore an alert expression like a mask while everyone patiently re-explained to Blascoe how the tool functioned, delicately avoiding pointing out that it was all Blascoe's fault.

Lucy came back into the room and paced around underneath Josh's desk, bumping into him with soft impacts. He steeled himself so he wouldn't glance at her—Josh had noticed that the distracted team members who were always shifting around and looking away and sipping coffee during their meetings didn't have their contracts renewed. Blascoe liked everyone staring straight ahead like news anchors.

Lucy whined.

This time Josh did look down. She was panting a little, drooling, even, and staring up at him with a beseeching expression.

Oh, surely, *surely* it wasn't happening *now*. The meeting would last about an hour and a half. Surely she could wait that long. He reached his hand down and she licked it. Her tongue felt dry and rough.

"Let's move on," Blascoe snapped, which was what he always said when he understood he'd screwed up. "Josh?"

Lucy stood up from under the desk and walked over by the front door. Josh took a deep breath, nodding. "Okay, we got the first results back from user tests on the front end," he stated neutrally. "We came in lower than expected in usability." *Actually, they hated the design, because of the stuff you put in there, Blascoe.* "I think I can explain why, though."

Lucy yipped in distress. Josh turned and stared at her. A fluid was puddled on the floor at her feet.

"How could that happen?" Blascoe demanded.

"I'm, uh, the problem . . . I have a chart . . . can you, can you hang on a second?"

"What?" Blascoe responded, sounding outraged. On the screen, everyone else shifted uneasily as Josh stood up and moved off camera. "Josh?" Blascoe called.

Lucy's eyes were imploring and pained. "Okay. Okay, Lucy," Josh soothed, trying to keep the fear out of his voice.

Lucy moaned, her legs trembling. Josh dashed back to his computer. "I have an emergency, I have to go," he said quickly, switching off the conference with a click of the mouse. Even in his panic, there was a momentary flicker of satisfaction at being able to put Blascoe out like a lightbulb.

Lucy was panting and pacing as Josh grabbed his keys and his wallet. *No.* This was *not* going to be a home delivery! "Let's go, Lucy!" he urged.

She didn't follow him. She lay down on the hardwood floor, her chest heaving. *Oh God.* "Everything is going to be all right," Josh told her. He ran to his pickup truck and opened the passenger door, his hands shaking, then dashed back into the house. Gingerly, he eased Lucy up, staggering a little under her weight. Her tongue lolled in her mouth. "Lucy! You okay? Lucy!" he hissed. Please, Lucy. *Please.*

He fumbled, trying to shut the front door of his house with his foot while still holding the dog, and then gave up and ran around and laid her as gently as he could across the front seat of his truck. The engine started right up. He glanced wildly at his open front door as he headed down the driveway, but decided it didn't matter—nobody ever came around, burglars or otherwise. "Good dog, good dog, Lucy." He stroked her head, and even in her obvious pain she managed to lick his hand. It pierced right through his alarm, that gesture, and he felt his heart heave in his chest. That she could feel affection for him under these circumstances gave him a fierce determination that nothing bad was going to happen. Not to Lucy. Not today.

Lucy panted and moaned while Josh bounced down the

rutted road. It occurred to him that he should have called ahead to let them know he was coming, but it was too late now—he'd left his cell phone in the drawer where it lived most of the time. His hands squeezed the steering wheel until his forearms trembled. "Oh please, oh please," Josh whispered over and over. He kept glancing anxiously at his companion, looking for what, puppies? And then what? He didn't know what to *do.* He'd never felt so helpless in his life.

He left his truck door open when he got to the vet's office, a small building just off North Turkey Creek Road. He picked up Lucy and ran with her in his arms, pounding and kicking at the front door of the vet's like the sheriff serving an arrest warrant. A stocky woman in her fifties flung the door back, staring at him as if he were crazy.

"She's in labor, but there's something wrong! She's crying and crying."

"Hey now. Slow down," the woman soothed.

"She was fine but then I took her temperature and it was under a hundred and her water broke, I mean, there was fluid. I was on a conference call and she went to the front door and there was a puddle." Josh tried to sound less hysterical, puffing rapid breaths through his cheeks.

"Why are you panting like that?"

"What?"

"Are you doing Lamaze breathing?"

"Of course not," Josh snapped, aware that he'd been doing exactly that. He deliberately slowed down, taking care with his words, though he pretty much wanted to scream at this woman. What did it matter what kind of breathing he was doing, she wasn't looking at the dog! "I am just trying to say I think there's something wrong. She seems in distress. I mean, look at her," he enunciated carefully.

Lucy's eyes were white-rimmed and her tongue hung from her mouth.

The woman finally stopped reacting to Josh's reactions and focused on Lucy, and her expression changed. "Let's get her back and let Dr. Becker have a look," she decided.

Dr. Becker was such a nice, calm, affable guy that Josh wanted to punch him. In Josh's opinion, everyone in the pet hospital should be wailing in terror. The vet's hands were gentle as they examined Lucy, who lay shivering on the table. "Was there a discharge?" he asked, looking at the wet fur on her legs.

"Yes, sir. On the floor," Josh replied.

"What color was it, did you notice?"

"Color?" Josh frowned, trying to remember, wishing everyone would stop talking and do . . . do *something* for poor Lucy. "I don't know. Green?"

"Green?" Dr. Becker glanced at him sharply, his blue eyes narrow behind his glasses. "You sure?"

"I . . . I don't know, I didn't really . . ."

"Don't worry about it, it's fine. You seem pretty upset," Dr. Becker observed.

"Hell yes, I'm upset! Who wouldn't be upset?" Josh shouted.

"That's okay, I understand. I'm just thinking that if I'm going to do what I'm going to do, maybe you should wait up front, would that be good with you? We may have a breech, here." Dr. Becker snapped on a pair of rubber gloves, nodding at his receptionist, who had magically appeared the moment Josh raised his voice.

"Why don't you come with me," she suggested in quiet, this-is-how-we-calm-mental-patients tones.

Seeing the gloves made Josh want to vomit, for some reason. He stumbled willingly after the woman. She pointed to a waiting area, but Josh couldn't imagine sitting there and reading *Bark* magazine, not just yet. He needed some air.

"Um, I left my truck door open," Josh told her. He pointed outside. "Okay if I . . . ?"

"Sure, of course."

Josh pushed through the office door and walked on weak legs out to his truck. For the first time, he noticed that the air was much colder than it had been even just a few hours before—the clean taste of it on his tongue was sharp, his breath a gust of steam. He shut his door and then leaned against his vehicle, willing his heart rate to slow down. Dogs had puppies all the time. Otherwise there wouldn't be any dogs. Lucy was fine now, she was going to be fine. They were at the vet. Everything was okay.

He just couldn't shake the image of Lucy licking his hand in the front seat on their way in.

After half an hour of forcing himself to be calm, he returned to the office and the woman looked up with a sympathetic smile.

"Is it going to snow?" she asked.

"I don't know. It's weird. Really cold and humid."

"The temperature has been dropping all morning," she replied.

Yes, that's just what he wanted to talk about, the *temperature*.

"Dr. Becker's the best there is," she reassured, seeming to understand his mood. "Your dog will be fine."

She's not my dog, Josh didn't say.

FOUR

Over the next hour, Josh's assessment of the woman behind the counter evolved from "sergeant major in the marines" to "kindly aunt." Every time he glanced up at her she smiled at him in compassion. Almost anyone would be a little stern with a stranger trying to kick the door in, he reasoned, and Josh certainly hadn't been friendly toward *her*.

"When will we know something?" Josh asked her. She never got impatient with him asking his variations of this question.

"I'm sure Dr. Becker will be out as soon as he can," she assured him.

A woman came in with a cat in a soft-sided carrier. She sat far away from Josh in the waiting room. "I'm sorry, Dr. Becker's running late, we had an emergency this morning," the woman behind the counter told the woman with the cat.

The cat woman turned and stared appraisingly at Josh.

"Sorry," he apologized. She glanced away.

The hallway door opened and Josh leaped to his feet as if there had just been an explosion. "Hey there, Josh. Why don't you come on back," Dr. Becker suggested. Something in his voice made Josh seek out the sympathetic eyes of the woman behind the counter before he followed Dr. Becker down the hall and into an office.

"Lucy's fine," Dr. Becker reassured. "Come sit down."

It wasn't an examining room; they were in a small space with a desk and two chairs. Pictures of a couple of children and what looked to be five hundred pets adorned the bookshelf behind the vet as he eased himself into his chair. "She's sedated right now, but I'll let you go back and see her in a minute."

Josh held himself very still. He was noticing the care with which the vet was avoiding mentioning the puppies, and felt a sense of foreboding. Dr. Becker read something in Josh's expression and nodded.

"I'm afraid the pups were all stillborn."

"I see." Josh inhaled and exhaled, truthfully not knowing how he felt. His concern, he realized, was Lucy—the puppies had always been an abstraction. Even now, he was mostly just anxious for Lucy. How would she react when, after all the pain and the panic, she had no babies to take home with her? "Do you know, I mean, what happened?"

Dr. Becker was watching Josh's face. "I have to ask, what have you been feeding your dog?"

"Feeding? Oh, um . . ." Josh realized he needed to explain how he'd happened to possess Lucy, and did so quickly. The vet's expression softened as he told the story.

"Well, it's certainly been an interesting couple of days for you, hasn't it?" Dr. Becker remarked dryly. "I don't know this Ryan person, and Lucy's never been here before. She's not microchipped; we checked that. So her diet?"

"I bought this dog food that's supposed to be really good, Nature's Variety, but she's only been on it since I got her. I've been mixing it in with the food Ryan left me."

"Ah. Well, lots of things can contribute to fetal death, but poor nutrition is always the first place I look. The stuff your neighbor gave you comes in a fancy bag and frankly if you dumped out the contents and just fed your dog the bag, she'd be better off. I know what it says about the nutritional content, but if you were to take a pair of leather work boots, add a quart of crankcase oil, and toss in a big flake of straw, you could grind it all up and the nutritional analysis would show a reasonable level of protein, fat, and carbohydrates, none of it digestible. That's essentially what Lucy's been eating. Throw it away—the food you bought is excellent and will help her heal more quickly."

Josh pictured poor Lucy choking down the crap Ryan had been giving her and moved easily from there to a fantasy where he went over to Ryan's house and beat the man on the head. He took in a deep breath. "All right." He nodded.

Dr. Becker ran through how to take care of Lucy, and Josh listened carefully. "Keep her as quiet as possible for a week. Don't let her run around outside—leash only. She'll probably have discharge from her vaginal tract for up to three to four weeks. It should look like old blood, not bright red, and any greenish discharge may mean a retained placenta, so call me immediately. She may come into milk, you'll see it seeping from her teats—call me if that happens. Understood? Give her a small amount of water when she goes home, and after a half hour if she hasn't gotten sick, offer her a small amount of food. Her diet can return to normal after twelve hours. Any vomiting or lack of appetite, call me."

With effort, Josh unclenched his fists, which he'd knotted with his rising tension. *I'm not up for this. I'm going to fail.* "I don't know," Josh murmured.

The vet raised his eyebrows. "Which part? Just call me if you have problems."

"I've just never . . ." Josh shrugged.

"You'll do fine. Let's go see your dog."

Lucy was sleeping in a large cage in the back. When Josh poked his fingers in through the cage, she opened one wet, unfocused eye.

"I'm sorry about the puppies," the woman behind the counter told him when he returned to his seat. The woman with the cat was gone.

"Yeah, well," Josh replied.

"Lucy might act a little depressed for a while. Sometimes it helps to give them a stuffed toy or two to carry around and sleep with," she counseled, glancing over her shoulder as if she was saying something she wasn't supposed to.

"Oh. Got it."

"Is it snowing?"

"Not yet," Josh answered, peering out the window.

"October third," she muttered. "It was seventy degrees on Friday! Guess this means a white Christmas, anyway. Are you from here?"

"Yeah, I grew up in Evergreen," Josh told her.

"Crazy weather. We moved from Detroit, this is our first fall. I knew it would be cold but I had no idea it was going to change so quickly."

"Well, but this is really unusual, and anyway, it will warm up again. It snows and melts, snows and melts—we could get a foot on Christmas Eve and have it melt the next day. Even in February, the sun comes out all the time."

"The sun?" Her eyes, accustomed to the gray skies of a Michigan winter, were disbelieving.

Clearly the woman expected Josh to lead Lucy out to the truck, but after paying the bill Josh picked the dog up and held her to him, her fur brushing his face, as he carried her and laid her on the front seat. "Poor Lucy," he whispered softly. She went right back to sleep.

Josh started the truck and let it idle, the heater blowing cold air on high. He rubbed his hands together—man, it was cold!

A light, misting rain started to fall, some of it frozen into tiny seeds of ice that bounced off his windshield. He switched on his lights, and then turned on his wipers, which smeared the water into a sheet instead of wiping it away.

"Ice storm," Josh noted out loud. He switched the blower to the defroster and waited impatiently for the air to melt away the ice, a battle the truck lost for a good three minutes before the wipers finally worked. The hood, when he could see it clearly, was covered with a clear, dimpled glaze.

He dropped it into four-wheel drive and crept onto the road.

In Colorado, you can tell who has lived in the mountains for a while and who has just moved in—the newcomers are in the ditch. Josh kept his speed at twenty miles an hour and shook his head at people thundering past at fifty-five. Just because four-wheel drive allowed you to drive forward more reliably didn't mean you could *stop* any sooner than anyone else. The sky up ahead was lit with the crazily tilted headlights of vehicles that had slid off the pavement, as if someone were staging a Hollywood premiere.

It was actually easier going on the dirt road—his knobby tires bit through the ice down to the dirt underneath. Lucy raised her head when he stopped in the wide area at the top of his driveway. In the beams from the headlights he could see that some of the rain was struggling to turn into snow, and that the aspens, many spangled with golden leaves, were bending under the weight of the frozen water glassing their limbs.

He opened his car door and Lucy sat up—it wasn't easy for her. Josh stepped out and nearly went down—you could play hockey in his driveway. Lucy's door cracked like breaking wood when he opened it, ice fragments falling to the ground.

"Can you do this yourself? It's just that I'm worried I'll fall if I carry you," Josh explained to the dog.

Lucy gingerly stepped down, sniffing. Josh carefully picked his way across the ice rink that was his front yard.

Lucy's claws were fully extended as she followed him up the steps.

The front door to his house was wide open—he mentally replayed the last time he was here, when messing with the door had seemed too much trouble. Inside, it was *cold*. His floorboard heat was ticking and banging like mad but was totally ineffective against the gusts of winter air that had been blasting into the house all day.

Josh pulled Lucy's bedding out of the bedroom and set it up near the hearth. The fire only took about five minutes to start, the kindling dry from sitting inside all summer.

"It'll warm up, you want a blanket?" he asked Lucy awkwardly. He could see his breath inside his own house. She wagged her tail, a double thump, then stretched out with a sigh on the pillow. She *did* seem depressed. Would she want one of the chew toys, or was that stupid? He didn't have anything that even remotely looked as if it could serve as a substitute for a puppy. He'd go to town and get some stuffed animals tomorrow. Would that really work, though, to line up a bunch of fake dogs as if they were nursing, try to fool Lucy into believing she'd delivered live young after all?

Josh couldn't imagine what the poor dog was thinking. Just forty-eight hours ago she'd been living with Ryan, whose care boarded on criminally negligent. Feeding a pregnant animal that awful crap! Then she was dumped here with a man who'd never owned a dog before and didn't know anything about taking care of one, and within a few hours she went into painful labor and now didn't have any puppies to show for it. Josh knelt on the bedding and stroked her head. "You'll be okay, Lucy. Promise." The words tasted thin and hollow in his mouth. How did *he* know she'd be okay? She hadn't been okay so far.

Oddly, when it occurred to Josh to leave another message for Ryan, he stayed the impulse, though he couldn't put his finger on the reason why. He just didn't want to call him.

The wood box on the hearth wasn't really all that full—restocking it was a winter chore, and with October barely begun he wasn't ready to declare it winter just yet. The woodpile was out by the truck. Josh could either go out there now or face dealing with wet logs for his fire in the morning. He glanced over at the sleeping dog. Would she feel abandoned if he left her to resupply the wood box? His throat tightened a little at the thought. He pictured her raising her head to watch him leave, supposing that he was walking out on her forever. Like Serena, or Ryan.

But he did need to get firewood. With it this cold in the house the baseboard heat wouldn't be able to do the trick on its own. He was leaving but he was coming back, that was the difference. Sighing, he flipped on the spotlight. The night became a swirling swarm of ice and snow and rain—he could barely even see the woodpile.

Josh struggled into a heavy waterproof coat. Lucy heard the noise and looked at him questioningly. "You wait right here, Lucy. I won't be long. I promise I'm not deserting you. Honest."

The stairs had some snow on them but were no less treacherous than when they'd been black ice. Josh slid over to the woodpile, laughing at his lack of sure footing. He grabbed up an armload of small logs and, not laughing now, worked his way back up to his front door, glancing at his pickup as he did so.

He saw, but didn't register, the box. There was a cardboard box in the pickup bed, a box he hadn't put there.

Once safely indoors he dropped his burden with a heavy bang. "Whew!" he said. The logs were all coated on one side with a thin layer of ice. He put his hands up to the fire, which was just starting to push back against the cold a little. Otherwise, it was still freezing in the house. "You cold? You okay? Do you hurt?"

Lucy's expression suggested she'd be better off without all the annoying questions, but Josh couldn't help himself. He needed reassurance that he wasn't doing further damage to this poor animal.

The fire was beginning to crack and pop. Josh jabbed at it with his fire poker because that's what he always did. "You hungry, Lucy? Oh wait, just water for now." Josh, on the other hand, was suddenly starving. He went over to the front floodlights, intending to shut them off and then head into the kitchen to fix himself something to eat, but then he paused, frowning.

That box.

What was that box? In the spotlights, it looked to be about twice the size of the microwave oven in which Josh would heat dinner. And was that something written on the side?

He bent forward, squinting. Someone had used a black

marker to draw a few crude letters on the cardboard. The curtain of rain and snow mostly obscured his vision, but then a gust of wind would wipe it away long enough for him to eventually make out what it said.

4 THE VET

For the vet? Josh's truck had been parked right out in front of Dr. Becker's office. Had some lazy delivery person decided it was the vet's truck?

Josh wondered when it had been put there. Had the box been there when he went out to shut his truck door? No, he was absolutely sure it had not. Whoever stuck it in the back of his truck must have done so after that.

Much as he didn't want to go back out in the elements, Josh was just too curious to wait until morning. He checked on Lucy, who had resumed sleeping, then tromped back outside and picked his way to the truck. The box seemed to weigh no more than ten pounds, and was heavier in the bottom. The cardboard sides were glistening with an icy coating.

Josh made his way back to his house and shut the door. Lucy's tail thumped. "Let's just see what we've got here, Lucy."

He carried the box over next to the fire and set it on the floor, turning on the lamp next to his chair. The lid of the box resisted opening—it was literally frozen shut. He banged at it a little, finally breaking it loose, and leaned over to peer inside.

At first he wasn't sure what he was seeing, and then, when it came to him what he was looking at, Josh gasped in horror.

Lying huddled at the bottom of the box were five small, mottled bodies. Puppies. They were newborn puppies, motionless, pressed together in a tight pile.

"My God," Josh breathed.

And then, just like that, the lights went out.

FIVE

With the electricity gone, the only light in the house was the flickering yellow glow from the fireplace. The bottom of the box was deep in shadow, its contents barely visible. Could he be mistaken?

Josh reached inside and gingerly touched one of the furry little lumps. It was cold under his fingers. He sucked in his breath. This was just too much, too much to bear that someone would dump a litter of tiny puppies in a box in this weather, leave them to freeze to death in Josh's truck. How could this happen? Who would do such a thing?

Why me?

Would it distress Lucy to smell the dead newborns? Josh looked over to where Lucy was lying, but she was back to sleeping soundly. Josh touched the back of another puppy and it was equally cold, equally still. *Just great.*

And then, under his hand, Josh felt something impossible: the puppy stirred, moving slightly.

It was alive.

Josh went from self-pity to alarm in just a second. "Oh my God!" he cried. He picked up the puppy. Yes, it was alive, but so, so cold. What the barely moving creature needed was heat, but the house was still an icebox. Maybe some of the others were still living, too—he had to warm them up, he had to save the puppies!

Carefully clutching the tiny bundle to his chest with one hand, Josh reached out with the other and grabbed handfuls of kindling and threw it on the fire. The smallest twigs ignited instantly, flaring with a gratifying burst of heat. It wasn't enough, but the fire was all he had.

The next puppy in the box was alive. So was the next. Josh didn't hesitate, he thrust them up under his sweater, pressing them to his bare skin. They felt like snowballs against his chest. Three was about all he could manage to hold while still shoveling sticks into the fire. He went for his newspaper stack, crumpling balls one-handed and tossing them into the blaze. Each wad of paper left a black ghost of itself when it became ash, but before it did so, it gave up its energy in a puff of flame.

He was so close to the flames his face was hot and his sweater smelled ready to combust. The three puppies weren't moving much and hadn't made a sound and there were still two in the box.

"Here, here," Josh said. Moving in quick, shaky jerks, Josh laid the three newborns on the floor at his knees and then yanked off his sweater. Tenderly he wrapped all three in the sweater, hot side against their chilly bodies. Okay. He picked up the other two. They were alive! He held them against his bare skin. He'd do shifts, back and forth, two, then three, then two, then three. They were so tiny! He leaned into the dancing fire, letting the heat bake his chest. The two new pups were as freezing and unmoving as the first three, but even still, he could tell by their slight stirring that they were breathing. What if they died now, in his arms?

More newspaper. The fire was roaring but running out of fuel, his supply of sticks dwindling. Reluctantly, he tossed in a small log that was wet from melted ice. It made a sizzling sound.

The tiny dog crooked into his right arm moved its head, and Josh inhaled sharply. "Don't die," he whispered. "Please don't die. Please don't die."

He heard a peep, a tiny noise, and glanced down with a start at his sweater on the floor. It lay deflated and flat, the puppies no longer inside.

Josh jerked his head around wildly and saw Lucy watching him from her soft bedding. Pressed up against her side were the three puppies, and that's what he'd heard. They were feeding. She'd removed them from the sweater, somehow, and carried them to her pillow. Now she was nursing them. Giving them life.

"No *way*," Josh breathed.

It was a little cooler over where they were feeding than it was right in front of the fire, but Lucy's milk was warming the newborns from within.

After a moment, he stood and crossed over to the dogs. He found unoccupied teats and one at a time held out his tiny burdens until they instinctively fastened on the life-saving nipples with their teeny mouths.

Even over the roar of the fire, he could hear their sucking, and the peeping was more pronounced, little squeals from the puppies as they had their first meal in the world.

Lucy turned her muzzle to them, licking them occasionally with her long, pink tongue.

Josh allowed himself a few minutes to watch the miracle before he went back to the fire. The wind kicked up outside, more than one tree limb crashing to the ground as the elements ripped them down, but his concentration was so focused on warming the house that he registered the wild storm as nothing more than background noise.

Josh fed wood to the flames all night, awakening from his place on the couch every hour or so to toss in more logs. The heat was strong enough that he kicked off his socks and then his blankets around midnight, but it didn't do much to thaw the lasagna from the freezer that he had optimistically set on the hearth soon after Lucy began feeding the puppies. He congratulated himself on his ingenuity when he found a pot with a metal handle and put the lasagna inside and held the assembly over the flames with fire tongs, but that just meant he wound up eating Italian food that was black on the bottom and crunchy with ice crystals in the middle.

Dawn was impossibly bright, and Josh was up with it. Still no electricity. Outside everything was coated with a sheen of ice, leaves, and twigs all wrapped in mirrors. A big ponderosa—probably the largest tree on his lot—had shattered under the weight of the heavy frozen blanket and lay raw and splintered across Josh's driveway, blocking access and escape. Not that he would be going anywhere soon anyway. The roads would be impassable until the weather warmed up, and the thermometer on his deck told him the sun would have to find a lot more ambition if it was going to push the temperature above the current five below. Arctic air had arrived with this weather system.

The puppies were warm and dry to the touch, all sleeping, all alive. Lucy nuzzled his hand with her moist nose when Josh reached for them. There seemed to be a message in that nudge: *everything's fine, don't disturb the kids.*

His laptop still had juice, but without an Internet connection, he really couldn't work. When he thought to use his cell to e-mail Gordon Blascoe an explanation and apology for going off grid, he found the phone in the drawer, battery dead, useless. *Dude, you don't answer your cell phone?* Ryan had demanded.

Up here in the mountains Josh had found he could only get a signal if he tromped over to a rocky outcropping in the corner of his property. So no, he didn't answer his cell phone, because it never rang unless he was in town. He sent texts from his computer when he needed to.

Josh plugged the cell phone charger into the wall for when the power eventually came back on. Then he dragged out an iron pot, filled it with water, and placed it in the fire. That gave him a dozen hard-boiled eggs, which with the cornflakes and milk would make up the bulk of his diet until the utility company managed to get the electricity flowing. He'd never before considered how dependent he was on the microwave.

When the eggs were done he poured the water on some coffee grounds in a bowl and then drained the mix through a paper towel and it tasted reasonable enough. He pulled his couch closer to the fire and sat sipping almost-coffee and watching the puppies, who squirmed a little, but basically weren't moving.

They squealed, though, when Lucy abruptly stood up and went to the front door. Josh let her out into the frigid air, conscious of the arctic wind sweeping over his feet at puppy level. Lucy was gingerly picking her way across the yard, sniffing, so Josh shut the door and went to the puppies.

"She's coming back. Don't worry," he soothed. He pulled a blanket off the couch and covered them, but that didn't stop their upset squawking. Through the big front window he watched Lucy squat in the thin crust of snow, and she watched him back. When she was finished they met at the front door. Lucy went straight to the pups and gave him a pitying look before she pulled the blanket off with her teeth, settling down heavily. It looked to Josh as if she was lying directly on some of the newborns, but Lucy wiggled and they soon were all nursing again. She lowered her head and sighed with a weariness that Josh felt connected her with all the mothers in history.

Lucy had done it, she'd saved the puppies. All Josh had done was bring in the cardboard box.

When night came it was less like darkness falling than the fireplace seeming to gain strength. Josh read his book and watched Lucy, who ate a hearty meal and drank from her bowl twice before Josh covered himself and slept.

He awoke to the sound of falling water, but it wasn't rain—the day was hazy and much warmer and the ice was melting rapidly. Trees shook themselves free and stood back up in a cascade of diamondlike droplets. Many of the aspen leaves would never get the chance to show off their autumn colors—they lay on the ground, beaten down by the storm.

That was Colorado weather for you—give it a few hours and it would change.

The puppies were still alive, and thus far Lucy showed no signs of rejecting them. When Josh looked into her eyes he thought he could see self-satisfaction, a redemption from what she had left behind in the vet's office. "You're a good dog," he told her.

Still no electricity. Pockets of frigid air were holed up in the back bedrooms—when he opened a door it poured out like ice water. Good thing the couch was comfortable.

The power outage could last days. He needed food that didn't require cooking or refrigeration. *Tortilla chips & can of bean dip*, he wrote on a pad. *Peanut butter.* What else? *Potato chips.*

If Josh was ever going to drive down into Evergreen he'd need to clear the driveway of the ponderosa pine the storm had knocked down. "You'll be okay, Lucy," Josh promised as he put on his rubber boots. Lucy, nursing the newborns, didn't look too worried about it.

The chainsaw in the shed only coughed awake after Josh had nearly yanked his arm out of the socket trying to start it, but eventually he had it throttled up and ready to bite into the big pine tree that blocked his driveway. But when it came time to sink the saw's metal teeth into the thick trunk, Josh hesitated.

For most of his life, Josh had been too small to put his

arms around this particular tree. It had withstood many storms, and still sported a dark scar where his sister, Janice, had backed the car into it when she had her learner's permit. He'd leaned against it for support when his mother and sister drove off, following the moving van that was removing them from Josh's life. Now it was down, too old and proud to bend under the relentless buildup of heavy ice. Once he cut into it, it would cease to be a tree. He would stack the logs in the woodpile to season for next winter.

It felt like an old friend had died.

For Christmas, Josh's father had wound strings of blue lights around the trunk, maypole fashion, a tradition Josh had cherished and continued. The lights were waiting in a bag that Josh had impatiently pulled out a week ago—like his mother, Josh always decorated for Christmas early. The nails his father had pounded into the pine tree to support the lights now bristled like barbs on a wire—Josh took special care to avoid them with his chainsaw.

When he had finished cutting the trunk into segments, he wiped tears away from his eyes, glad no one could see him crying over a tree, of all things. Well, not no one: Lucy was watching him from the window. He went over to let her out, and she quickly squatted before returning to the house.

What a great dog! Somehow having her made him feel better, less alone.

He recalled that the vet had said not to let her run loose, but so far the orphan pups were turning out to be the most effective leash possible.

The ponderosa logs were heavy—he grunted as he carried

them across the soggy yard and stacked them at the end of the woodpile. He'd split them next fall.

He was tired and sore when he finished, but at some point while he was outside the electricity had come on, and after eating a microwaved beef dinner, Josh was able to take a hot shower to soothe his aches. Later he went around the house turning off lights that he'd irrationally switched on when there was no power.

No Internet yet, nor landline, but the cell phone soon had enough juice stored up for him to make a call. He put his boots back on and squished his way to the high point on his property where crumbling rocks jutted up out of the soil in a mound that was round and dry like an old man's elbow. He left a message for Gordon Blascoe, explaining where he'd been the past couple of days, hoping that the odd dead sound didn't imply that the message wasn't recording. He checked and saw that he barely had a signal, and then called Ryan's number.

"The number you have dialed is not in service," a man's voice lectured, crackling and popping with static. Josh didn't know if he was annoyed or relieved.

The vet's office returned a fast busy signal, which meant their service wasn't restored yet, either. Who knew how long that would take?

He went back to the house and looked at Lucy, who wasn't lying with her puppies. "Lucy, you want to come over here?" he asked, patting the pillow where the puppies were in a row as if lined up at a cafeteria. Lucy just looked at him with a *you think it's such a great place you lie there for a while* expression. It was what Josh had been afraid of—she was having second thoughts about her adoptive family.

He headed back outside to the rocky outcropping. Taking a breath, he called information, and was connected to the animal rescue in Evergreen.

"Animal Rescue, this is Kerri," a woman answered.

"Hi, Kerri, my name is Josh Michaels," Josh greeted, clearing his throat.

"This is a pretty bad connection," she noted.

"Yeah, sorry about that. So the reason I'm calling, I have a situation I need help with."

"Uh-huh," Kerri answered slowly. "Tell me."

Josh quickly explained everything: how Ryan had dumped his ex-girlfriend's dog on him, and how he'd come to have puppies that didn't belong to him.

"Wow, that's an amazing story," Kerri marveled.

"Yeah."

"So how can I help you, Josh?"

"Oh. So, I guess I need to turn them in."

"I'm sorry?"

"You know. I need to bring the puppies in. Drop them off."

SIX

I don't understand what you're saying to me," Kerri responded. Her voice had grown cold.

"Um . . ." Josh groped for a way to make himself more clear.

"You want to bring the newborn puppies here to the shelter?"

"Yes."

"I don't get it," she replied, obviously angry. "Why don't you save a trip into town and just kill them yourself?"

"What?" Josh gasped. "What do you mean, kill them myself? What are you talking about?"

"Yeah, you do know we'd have to euthanize them immediately, don't you? We don't have the resources to hand-feed five babies around the clock. *You* do, but apparently it's too much of a hassle for you."

"I do," Josh repeated stupidly.

"It takes a lactating female willing to adopt them, which you just told me you had."

"But won't she eventually figure out the dogs aren't hers?" Josh asked.

"So?"

"So, I mean . . . I saw this thing one time about wolves,

and when they figured out the cubs didn't have their DNA, the adults killed them."

"And that's why you want to bring the puppies to us."

"Sure, yeah, that and I thought that I had to. I mean, legally. I know it can't be legal to have six dogs living in your house unless you're a breeder. I thought, abandoned dogs, you're supposed to call the shelter. I would have called the vet but his line's still down."

"You're worried about the puppies, *that's* why you want to bring them in. Not because you're the biggest creep in America." Kerri sounded relieved.

"Won't she abandon them when she senses they're not her puppies?" Josh fretted.

"You know, I guess she could, but I've never heard of it happening. We had a lactating dog here one time who nursed two kittens for us."

"No way."

"Seriously. I mean, maybe the alpha male wolf would kill cubs that weren't his, I don't know about that, but your dog isn't going to hurt those puppies."

"She's sort of acting, though, like she's rejecting them." Josh described how just moments ago Lucy had refused to return to her pillow.

"You think maybe she's just tired of taking care of them? Wouldn't you need a break?"

"I thought they liked it. You always hear about mothers getting this endorphin release when they nurse their babies."

"Five of them?" Kerri challenged, laughing.

Josh had time to think of a reply as a storm of static interrupted their conversation. Unfortunately, all he could come up with was "Oh."

"And you're allowed to have a litter of puppies. You're right, the county limits you to three dogs, but you have something like six months to adopt them out."

"Huh."

"You don't sound happy," Kerri observed, her voice turning chilly again.

"It's just . . . I've never had a dog before in my life and I don't know how to take care of one and now I have a half dozen of them. The vet says that the reason the puppies were stillborn was because they ate crappy dog food. I've got good dog food, but what else am I doing wrong, you know? I don't have Internet back up yet, so I can't even research it. Like, it looks sometimes like Lucy's lying right on top of the babies," Josh explained, putting his finger on what had been causing him the most anxiety. "Am I supposed to maybe line them up for her or something?"

Kerri laughed. "No, they're fine. I'm glad that you're worried you're not doing the right things, though. That means you'll take good care of them. Call us any time; we can help you with all your questions, or tell you when we think you should contact the vet. And if you're willing to foster the puppies, we'll take care of adopting them to their forever homes for you."

Josh told her that would be great and Kerri took down his address and said someone would be out to see him in a few days. "Are the roads clear up where you are? I'm hearing there are still rockslides and downed trees all over. Crazy weather."

"I haven't been out on the roads yet," Josh told her. "I was going to head into town soon."

"Might be best to wait until tomorrow, you could get stuck sitting on the road while the county clears a rockslide," Kerri advised.

After they hung up Josh discovered she was right: standing on the rocks at his connectivity corner and surfing with his cell phone, he found that the road crews were all out clearing rocks and cars and that people were asked not to venture out unless it was strictly necessary. Josh spent the day watching the puppies. Now that he knew Lucy wasn't going to reject the newborns, he found it easy to just sit and stare at the tiny dogs as they squeaked and nuzzled each other and their mommy.

When awake they were in a constant scrum, blindly pushing against each other for no apparent reason, or feeding with gusto while Lucy gazed raptly down at them. Asleep, they sprawled motionless, always lying pressed against their siblings for reassurance.

His Internet connection was back up the next morning. Reading backward from the moment his electricity went out, he found e-mails from Gordon Blascoe demanding to know where he was, followed by chatter from his team members who figured out what was going on and deduced that Josh wouldn't be back online for a few days. Several people expressed hopes that Josh would be okay; Blascoe was not among them.

Josh sighed when he saw the direction the project had taken. He hadn't been able to upload his report, which meant that Blascoe didn't have the benefit of Josh's analysis of the problems that had surfaced during user testing of the new interface. They were now all focused on the wrong solution because they didn't fully understand the issues. People wanted simple; Blascoe was one of those geeks who thought the way to make something better was to keep piling on functionality until it was so complicated no one wanted to use it.

What to do now? If he sent his report, it would save his clients a lot of time and effort, but it would also make it clear that Blascoe's tendency to rush to decision—"Blascoe's Blunders"—had steered them wrong. Probably it was not a good idea to point out that the project manager had done something stupid. Though to be fair, nothing in the report directly *said* that: you'd have to be a careful reader to distill that message, and Blascoe wasn't known for paying a lot of attention.

In the end, he sent it, along with a meticulously worded e-mail apologizing for being off grid and stating that his analysis wasn't intended to say that Blascoe had been wrong, even though that's exactly what his analysis was intended to say.

Barely had he pushed "send" when he heard the crunch of a vehicle coming up his driveway. He looked out to see a mud-spattered Subaru wagon swing around next to his truck and stop.

A woman a few years younger than Josh stepped out, shaking her long brown hair. She wore jeans and a plaid shirt in a way that attracted Josh's attention in a most favorable fashion. She stomped her feet as she came onto his front deck.

Josh heard her knock from the bathroom, where he was frantically brushing his teeth. "Coming!" he shouted. He yanked on a clean shirt. Lucy was watching him alertly as he opened the door.

"You Josh?" the woman asked, offering a generous smile that reached into her deep blue eyes.

"Yeah. Yes, yes I am. Josh Michaels," Josh responded.

She held out a hand and he took it—her fingers were warm as they shook. "I'm Kerri, from the shelter? I know I said a couple of days, but I just couldn't wait to see them."

He invited her in and she immediately crossed over to where Lucy lay on the floor. "Puppies!" she sang happily. Lucy wagged her tail and Kerri stroked her head. "Such a good dog, good dog. Is it okay if I touch your puppies, mommy dog?"

"That's Lucy," Josh introduced. He blinked in surprise as she picked up a black and brown and white puppy. "Wow!" he exclaimed.

"Oh, you are so cute, look how darling you are," she crooned. She glanced at Josh. "Wow?"

"I didn't know I was allowed to pick them up. I thought maybe, I don't know, if I got my scent on them, Lucy might . . ." Josh shrugged.

"Kick them out of the nest? Refuse to give them worms?" Kerri teased. She grinned at him and Josh could feel himself grinning back so widely it stretched his cheek muscles.

"Right, well, I told you, I never had a dog before," he apologized.

"Good mommy, Lucy," Kerri praised, setting the puppy back down. "See how this one is smaller than the others?" Kerri asked, pointing to an all black and brown dog. "You need to make sure she suckles two separate teats every day. Like this." Kerri held the tiny puppy to a vacant teat, and the newborn obligingly began to feed. "Look how the tiny little tongue is sliding forward, that means she's got a good grip and is feeding real well."

"She?"

"Yes. Let's check the others." Kerri pulled each puppy away and held them up. Lucy watched her carefully, but didn't seem to object. "Three boys and two girls," Kerri announced.

Josh realized he was watching her bend over with considerable approval, and raised his eyes quickly when she turned to him—but not quickly enough to completely get away with it. Something flickered in her expression. Speculation? Josh felt his face grow warm.

"I think you've got boxer/Lab/something going on here. The coloring is right for boxer, all white and brown and black, but the fur's a little long and the faces are like Labrador faces. We'll be able to tell more when they're older." She gave the one she was holding a kiss on the nose. "Won't we? We'll know more when you are a great big puppy," she crooned in baby talk. "Okay, back you go to Mommy."

Kerri told him that having the dogs lying out on a pillow and a blanket by the fireplace was not ideal. "You're going to need a box, something the mom can step out of. Are you handy?"

"Handy? Meaning, here?"

"No." Kerri laughed. "I don't mean are you handy like, are you around, I mean handy as in able to build things. Most guys who live in the mountains are either good at building things or shooting stuff." Her eyes glanced over at the single shotgun on his gun rack.

"That's in case of bears. It's got a salt load," Josh explained hurriedly. He didn't think a woman who worked at a rescue shelter would be keen on someone who hunted animals. Josh had never shot at anything living.

"So, no shooting. How about building stuff?"

"Yeah." Josh straightened, pushing his chest out a little. "I can do that."

Kerri sketched out what the ideal box would look like, with a place to play and a chamber to sleep in. "These little rascals won't do much for about three weeks, but then all of a sudden they'll be on the move. Mom's hair falling out yet?"

"Her hair?"

"It will. Sometimes it's in clumps and sometimes so you won't even notice it. Don't be alarmed. I brought some vitamins to put in Lucy's food, and an instruction booklet. What do you do for a living?"

"Oh." Josh looked at his computer. "I do contract graphic user interface design and implementation."

"Okay, no idea. Computers?"

"Right."

"So then this will be a completely different experience for you, won't it?"

Josh nodded. "Yeah."

"You don't sound excited."

"I'm just worried I'll mess up."

"No, you'll be great. Besides, I'll help." She gave Josh another sunny smile. He pictured Kerri coming out to his house a few times a week. They'd laugh, take Lucy for walks, play with the puppies. He saw the two of them sitting in front of the fireplace, drinking wine. She'd smile that smile at him, toss her hair like the first time he saw her, he'd reach for her. . . .

"So," Kerri said, walking right through his fantasy to the fireplace, where she grabbed a picture of Amanda off the mantel and showed it to him. "Who's this?"

SEVEN

Josh took far, far too long to answer her question, his brain frozen in something akin to panic. Finally he cleared his throat.

"Amanda," he said faintly.

"Amanda," Kerri repeated. She looked at the picture, then back at Josh.

"Wife?"

"Oh, no. I've never been married."

"Girlfriend, then."

Josh nodded mutely.

Kerri set the picture down and examined the others. Josh was uncomfortably aware of just how many of them were of Amanda. "This blond girl with the man and children must be your sister? And her family?"

"Yeah. Janice."

"Josh and Janice."

"Janice is youngest."

"Nice-looking family."

"Thanks. The boys aren't hers," Josh remarked, wincing inwardly at the way he'd put it. He'd wanted to explain how his little sister could have three boys over the age of ten, but he was off to a bad start. "I mean, it's her husband's second marriage. She's a good mother, though," he ended awkwardly.

"That's good," Kerrie noted, smiling at him.

Josh glanced back at Amanda's picture, thinking maybe he needed to provide an explanation.

"So, what're you feeding Lucy?" Kerri asked.

"Um, Nature's Variety. Got a dog on the bag?"

She laughed. "They *all* have a dog on the bag."

"I mean," Josh started to explain, then stopped himself. *I mean a healthy-looking dog,* he'd been about to say. As distinguished from what, the bags that featured sick dogs?

"In about three weeks, you'll start with a little solid food for the babies. Stick with that brand, it's great. Add a little water to the canned food to make it even softer. Most people say no cow's milk, so I'd stay away from it. Let them sort of suck the food off your fingers a little, then set out small amounts. Try to make sure they each get some. Any questions, you can call me."

"Sure, let me get your number." Josh crossed to his laptop and popped open his address book. When he looked at her, she had her arms crossed and was gazing at him appraisingly. "What?" he asked.

"You already have the number for the shelter. You called, remember?"

"Oh. Right." Josh kept the disappointment from bleeding into in his voice. He glanced down and his inbox told him he had a message from Gordon Blascoe, subject line, "Your contract."

With a sinking feeling, he clicked it open. It was a typical Blascoe Blurt. "Please prepare a final invoice for the week ending Oct 7. We are terminating your contract."

"What's wrong?" Kerri asked.

Blinking, he looked up at her. "Oh. Nothing. Well, not nothing. I just got fired."

"Fired?" she repeated, shocked.

"Yeah."

"In an e-mail? Not even with a phone call?" she demanded.

"No, that's pretty much how they do it."

"That's terrible!" Kerri's cheeks flushed and her eyes narrowed, as if it were happening to her. "What kind of people fire you with an e-mail?"

"It's because I'm an independent contractor."

"I don't care what you are, people can't just fire you like that. Did you do something?"

"I sent in a report that made the boss look like he'd made a mistake."

"And they fired you. For that. It sounds like you were just doing your job, they can't fire you for doing your job. Is there someone you can complain to?"

Josh realized he was enjoying how angry she was on his behalf. He told her that this was the way it worked, in his world. "It started with the dog, in fact. Lucy went into labor while we were in the middle of a conference," he informed her, maybe bragging a little.

"Do they know that?"

"They wouldn't care."

"That's terrible. So you're out of work."

"Looks like."

"Will you be able to find a job? I mean, Christmas is like two months away, I can't imagine people do much hiring during the holidays," Kerri asked, going from furious to concerned.

"Sure. Yes. Maybe not immediately, but I'll be okay."

Her gaze lingered on him long enough for him to feel himself flush again. Maybe he should ask her to stay for dinner. He probably could thaw something appealing.

Kerri abruptly turned away. "I need to get going." She walked to the door and opened it herself before he could do so. "Did you tell the vet about the puppies?"

"Yes, I called and he kind of said what you did, which is that everything sounded like it was working out."

"Right, then," she replied. He followed her down the steps and up to her car.

"Maybe we could . . . ," he started to say. Kerri slipped into her car, shutting the door, and then sliding her window down when her engine was running.

"You know where the shelter is, right?"

"Sure, I've seen it."

"Great! Bye." Kerri backed around and then bounced down the rutted driveway. He watched her go, his hand up in a wave for if she looked back, but she didn't.

You know where the shelter is, right? That sounded like she wanted him to visit her. *You already have the number for the shelter. You called, remember?* That sounded like she wasn't interested in having him call her personally, but only as part of a business transaction.

Interested or not? Which was it?

Kerri had put the photograph of Amanda in the wrong place and Josh slid it back to where it belonged. It was taken the day he realized he was in love with Amanda. She was sitting on a rock in the sun by Bear Creek, her blond hair turning almost white in the sunlight.

"You're such a man-child," Amanda had teased him before she posed for the picture. Her laugh was gentle and warm. He had just explained to her how, when he threw away socks, he always tied them together in a knot.

"They've been mated all that time, so I tie them so they'll never be apart. I'd hate to think of them lying there at the dump, each one wondering where the other one was."

"Man-child" sounded so loving coming out of her mouth, then. Later, though, it somehow changed, became more of a complaint. How could something she initially thought adorable turn bad, like a piece of fruit gone sour?

Josh sighed. Kerri stirred something long dormant within him, and it felt good, alive. So yeah, he should have explained about Amanda. He had just been caught off guard.

Lucy was giving him an appraising look.

"What? I had to let her leave," he protested defensively.

Lucy glanced out the window, then back at him, communicating what Josh felt was clear disappointment. "Of course, sure," he agreed. If he'd thought about it, he would have had a lunch or something ready, would have asked her out to coffee, but to be fair he hadn't expected her and, well, he hadn't expected *her*, hadn't expected that the voice on the other end of the telephone call would be attached to someone so pretty.

He had Kerri in mind when he built the box, thinking he would impress her with how handy he was with his carpenter skills. He even considered a tongue and groove design, though in the end decided not to do that because he really didn't know how. When he was through with the project, he had a large, flat box with eight-inch sides that was separated into two chambers by an eight-inch-high partition that could be partially removed. The smaller chamber he filled with a soft quilt from the attic, the larger one he lined with newspapers. He smiled, envisioning removing the central partition and letting the puppies run out and play in the larger area, though at this point they weren't doing any running or playing or even moving.

Lucy was completely unimpressed with the box, but seemed to comprehend what was intended when Josh carried the puppies back there and put them on the quilt. "This is where you feed them now, Lucy. They can't get out until they're a lot bigger."

Josh took a picture of the box to show Kerri.

It felt strangely dislocating to be off Blascoe's project. He found himself thinking about it often, of items on his task list left unchecked, pondering solutions to problems that were no longer his to solve.

Will you be able to find a job? I mean, Christmas is like two months away, Kerri had asked. More like two and a half months, but she did have a point. He needed to get work before the high-tech world put on silly hats and started spending every day at holiday parties. Josh opened his address book and plugged himself into his social media contacts and began launching inquiries. Anyone hiring? Starting a new project? Need a new web- or PC-based interface?

The answer seemed a dismal no, but he kept trying. He updated his résumé and it looked good. Something would come up soon.

Two days later, Josh was sitting in his pickup truck, gazing at the front entrance of the rescue shelter. In the mountains, towns tended to crowd into the narrow valleys cut by rivers fighting their way down to the flatlands, and Evergreen was no exception, its main street shouldered with buildings on either side that backed up into the rock face on the left and the creek on the right. Away from the downtown, though, the hills were more friendly and round. This gave the shelter room in the back for dog runs, and the storefront window had been decorated with hand-painted cartoon dogs and cats. *Coming*, a banner proclaimed, *The Dogs of Christmas.*

He pictured himself entering the shelter and asking for Kerri. He'd tell her he wanted to get her approval on the construction of the box. He'd show her the photograph on his cell phone and she'd like how handily he'd built it. Then he'd somehow steer the conversation toward buying her lunch. Maybe as thanks for designing the box—that could be the excuse. Or maybe he'd look at his watch and be surprised that it was lunch time and ask her if she'd join him. He could tell her he had more questions about the puppies and ask her if they could discuss them over a meal, maybe. He'd better come up with some questions, in that case. Or he could say, "It's such a nice day, want to grab lunch at the golf club?"

A bell rang when Josh opened the front door. "Hey there!" Kerri greeted, coming from somewhere in the back. She wore a red fleece jacket unzipped over a light gray wool sweater and her thick hair was pulled back in what Josh thought was probably still called a ponytail. He normally didn't like ponytails but was willing not to take offense to this one.

Josh wore clean jeans and a pressed collared shirt that he'd picked after trying on everything he owned.

"Hi, Kerri."

"You here to take me to lunch?" Her blue eyes sparkled at him playfully.

He almost groaned at how easy it was. "Yeah. Exactly."

They walked out to his truck. He cleared his throat. "It's such a nice day, want to grab lunch at the golf club?"

"Sure."

They sat on the balcony at the club, which was open to the public. He ordered a burger and so did she, which made him feel that they had a lot in common. The aspens had fought back against the ice storm and were gradually paling yellow, so it was back to looking like a normal autumn day, warm and glorious.

"Supposed to be like this all week," Kerri said, reading his mind. He liked how she could do that. "So, you still fired? No appeal?"

"Yeah. Yes. But I'll get another job soon," Josh stated firmly. He didn't want to come across as some jobless guy who wouldn't be able to pay for their food.

"You're just so calm about it. Not an emotional guy," Kerri observed.

"No, I . . ." Josh didn't like the idea that she would think he was some robot without feelings. "That isn't true, at all. I have lots of feelings about stuff."

"Really? Like what kind of stuff?"

"You know," he replied uncomfortably. "Emotional stuff."

Kerri laughed, her teeth flashing at him. "Fine, name one."

"Name one what?"

"Time you were emotional. Like when . . . no, you tell me."

He wondered what she'd been about to say. "So, like . . ." She waited while he tried to force something to come out of his mouth. Did he want to tell her that Lucy nursing the puppies warmed his heart and that he was spending hours of his days sitting and watching it like a TV show? Well, but that wasn't a feeling, really. Anger was a feeling, but even he was smart enough to know that women didn't exactly treasure anger in a man. Sad was a feeling—he'd bet that was the kind of emotional stuff she was looking for.

She was watching him and he felt a rising panic. Lots of stuff made him sad, like . . . like . . . . "The tree," he blurted.

She nodded thoughtfully. "Maybe you should tell me just a little more," she encouraged.

He told her about the proud old ponderosa pine that had

been felled by the ice storm. How he always wound blue lights around it for Christmas. How cutting that tree into pieces had moved him deeply. He didn't say he cried, but he confessed to feeling really sad. That was emotional, right? "I just remember that tree from when I was a kid. And now it's gone."

"So, wait, that's the house you grew up in?"

"Yeah."

"Did you like, inherit it from your parents?"

"No, both of my parents are still alive. My dad lives in England and has a whole new family. His son, my step-brother, is twelve years younger than I am—just turned sixteen. Then there's a ten-year-old and eight-year-old twins, all girls. I don't see them very often. Like, it's been since just after the twins were born. England is a long way." *And it's not my family, not really,* Josh didn't add.

"Wow." Kerri glanced up, smiling, as the waitress set their plates down in front of them. Josh could look at that smile all day long.

"My mom lives in Florida and it's the opposite," Josh continued. "Her husband is retired, and his son, who is also my stepbrother, is in his forties, almost twice my age. They don't budge from their condo, so if I want to visit I have to go there."

"So how did you wind up with the house?"

"At first my dad hung on to it—there was always this idea that he'd come back to visit all the time, back to see his kids, I mean. But London's so far, you know, it was harder to make it work than he'd thought it would be. Then we put most of our stuff in storage and tried to rent it, but that was pretty hit-or-miss. I was supposed to look after the place for a percentage of the rent, though I was away at school, so that plan didn't go so well, either. Then after college I got a programming job in Golden."

"Right down the hill," Kerric observed.

"Exactly. Property values had dropped, and Dad said if I took over the payments, I could have the place, so . . ." Josh shrugged.

"How long ago was this?"

"That we did the paperwork? I guess maybe four years ago."

"And your sister is . . ."

"Janice, yeah. Portland, Maine. Husband, two kids, boys. When I talk to her she's always going to soccer or hockey or something. I get up there even less. We weren't close growing up."

"It's just really interesting that you bought the house you grew up in. I don't think I've ever met anyone who has done that."

"Yeah . . ." Josh shrugged, feeling like he ought to explain himself to her even though he couldn't really explain himself to himself. Instead he changed the subject. "And how about you, did you grow up here?"

"Here, in the mountains? No, but down in Denver. I always wanted to live here and then one day I just moved. My mom's in rehab right now, which is a good thing that we all hope works this time. I was a little surprise that came along during a time when she *wasn't* in rehab, so she sort of lost track of who the dad might be." Kerri regarded him archly, as if challenging him to judge her for her background. But he just couldn't stop gazing at those blue eyes of hers, and gradually a bit of pink burned its way onto her cheeks.

"What is it?" she asked.

"Nothing. I'm sorry about your mom. I mean, it must be hard."

"Sure. But life is hard, right? I mean, we've all had to endure stuff at some point. You can't escape it, it's part of being human."

"Exactly."

"Speaking of that," Kerri continued slowly. She swirled her spoon in her iced tea, focused on the tinkling ice, then raised her eyes to his.

"Yeah?"

"Amanda," she said softly. Kerri's eyes were warm with sympathy.

Okay, here it comes. Josh nodded, ready to talk about it. "How did she die?"

EIGHT

H aving Kerri ask how Amanda died was oddly as if Josh had just heard that Amanda *did* die. His stomach gave a kick and turned cold.

And why did she even wind up with that impression? He tried to think of what he might have said to imply such a thing. Could his expression really have been so mournful when Kerri had asked him about the blonde in the photograph that Kerri could only conclude Amanda was dead?

He flashed back to the awkward and insufferable night at the Little Bear Saloon, when he'd given Ryan his phone number. Did *Ryan* think Amanda was dead? Was that why he said that Josh was "lucky"?

Kerri was watching him intently, and he had the sense that she was close to reaching out to touch his hand. "Uh, she's not."

Kerri's face showed noncomprehension.

"Dead," Josh elaborated. "Amanda's not dead."

Kerri blinked. "Oh." She sat up, considering this, and then regarded him sharply. "So she's coming back?"

God, what a question. "I mean," he started, sorting through his thoughts, "It's more like she's . . ." He shrugged.

"You said she was your girlfriend," Kerri stated, sounding like a prosecutor at trial. "*Is* she your girlfriend?"

"We were together for four years."

"So you broke up? How long ago?"

"Like, the morning of April tenth."

Kerri's laugh was humorless. "The morning of April tenth; do you remember what time?" She held up her hand. "Don't answer that."

"Of course I don't remember the time," Josh protested.

"You were living together? In your place?"

Josh nodded.

"And she moved out, and you kept this shrine to her? Who does that?"

"A shrine? It's not a shrine. Look, wouldn't it be childish to throw all her pictures away, just because we broke up? We're still friends."

"She live here?"

"Here in Evergreen? No, she moved to Fort Collins."

"Which is maybe two hours away, right? How often do you go up for a visit?"

"I haven't." Josh looked out onto the golf course, watching without seeing as two men walked by with their clubs.

"She go up there because of a man?" Kerri's voice had lost its sharp edge.

Josh nodded, swallowing.

"Then, Josh, no, it's not childish. Your girlfriend and you broke up and now she's with someone else. You put her pictures in a cardboard box because it's over, you don't keep them all over the place, you don't keep her perfume in your bathroom cabinet, you don't sleep in the bedroom down the hall instead of the room you shared because you can't bear it—you move on."

Josh gazed back at her. For some reason her face was flushed and her eyes wide, as if they were having a fight or something. "You looked in my bathroom cabinet?"

Her hand briefly touched her mouth. "Oh." She lowered her eyes to her food. "Yeah, sorry. I just . . . right, look, I seem to have a talent for finding men with substance abuse issues, maybe because my mom made me blind to it. And I met you and I thought finally here's a normal guy instead of someone all emotionally damaged, or an addict, or both. But I needed to check because usually the first I find out about it is one day I stumble upon all these pills—prescription, of course, all with prescriptions." Her mouth twisted as a bitter memory came and went. "So I just thought I'd cut to the chase. I get that it was wrong and everything."

A small smile twitched onto Josh's lips. *A talent for finding men,* she'd said. He liked the way she'd put that, like he was a man that she had found.

"Sorry. I know it's not my business," she apologized.

He felt pretty good about the whole conversation, needing only to clear up one misunderstanding. "And the reason I don't sleep in my parents' room is just because I like to sleep in my room, where I grew up," he explained. "I like opening my eyes and seeing the dent I put in the ceiling with a *Star Wars* saber, and looking out at the same trees."

This sounded perfectly reasonable to Josh, but she was looking oddly at him. "What?" he finally asked.

"I'm just thinking I can't imagine having such a wonder-ful childhood that I'd want to relive any part of it," Kerri said simply.

Now Josh wanted to reach out and touch *her* hand. Before he could act on the impulse, she pulled it away and looked at her watch. "I need to go." Kerri signaled to the waitress.

"Um . . ." Josh just didn't want this to be over yet. "Want to walk around the lake? It's such a pretty day. Just, like, for a few minutes?" he suggested desperately.

"Fine," Kerri agreed, shrugging like it was nothing.

The waitress set the bill in front of Kerri and Josh grabbed it as if snatching a pistol away from a child. "Thanks for lunch," Kerri said, smiling.

Evergreen Lake would have been called a pond in most other states, but in water-starved Colorado, if you couldn't empty it with a bucket, it was a lake. Enthusiasts fished and canoed the forty acres of cold water, and only a local ordi-nance kept people from running power boats on the thing. A barely perceptible breeze was enough to stir the sun's reflec-tion into dancing sparkles as they walked the path encir-cling the green water, Josh keeping his pace slow to make the time last as long as possible. They talked about the pup-pies, which as far as Josh was concerned was better than discussing Amanda but not nearly as interesting as this idea that Kerri had a talent for "finding" the wrong sort of men but that, in Josh, she had *not*.

Josh had met Amanda as a set-up, a *have I got a girl for you* thing that his friends Wayne and Leigh put together. Josh remembered driving over to his friends' house, full of dread, knowing the night would be the worst on record. Leigh thought that just because she made Wayne happy, Josh only needed a girl and then he'd be happy, too. She'd brushed away Josh's protests that he already was happy: he didn't have a girlfriend, so, in Leigh's mind, he must be miserable.

Leigh seemed to have an endless supply of friends for whom Josh would be perfect (and vice versa), though previous attempts had missed perfection by a considerable measure.

Amanda was standing by the fireplace in the small living room, talking to Wayne in a forced-casual fashion, as if they hadn't all been waiting tensely for Josh to pull in the driveway. Josh entered the house carrying a bottle of wine and was giving Leigh a glare, trying to frown the manic enthusiasm from her face, when Amanda turned around and Josh's heart froze in his chest.

That's how Josh knew how to meet women: Leigh would find them and Wayne would say his wife was driving him crazy and that Josh needed to come over for dinner so Leigh would shut up about it. The girl would be at the fireplace and would hit perfection one hundred percent with a single glance.

What Josh didn't know how to do was turn this wonderful afternoon into the start of something more. He must have appeared pretty weak to Kerri with his sad tale of being dumped by another woman and having his heart broken by a tree; how was he supposed to repair the damage and get it to the point where they went on a date?

"Now I really, really have to get back to the shelter," Kerri finally announced. Josh hid his look of disappointment and they reversed direction. *Okay, back at the truck,* Josh decided. He'd open the door for her, so they'd be pretty close, and he'd ask her out to dinner. Or coffee, would dinner be too aggressive? They'd had lunch, but with her giving him all kinds of advice about the puppies, now it felt less like a date and more like a meeting, or something.

"No, don't bathe them, Lucy is keeping them clean, don't worry," Kerri was saying as they approached the vehicle. Why couldn't Josh think of anything to ask about except dog stuff? "Great day," he observed, not for the first time that afternoon. There, that was it: dogs and the weather. That's all he was capable of discussing. He would never have another girlfriend in his life. Why go on a date with Josh Michaels? It was easier just to stay home with your dog and watch the weather channel.

He'd parked a little close to the utility pole, and he fretted now over what that would mean. If he tried to get between her and the pole, he'd be crowding her, but if he stood on the other side of the pole it might block the whole conversation, which was going to be tough enough as it was since he *still had no idea* what he was going to say.

"Hey, the door on your side can be a little tricky, I'll get it for you," Josh told her as they crunched across the gravel. He'd meant to make the offer but it was too early, they were still forty feet from the pickup. The part about the door being sticky wasn't even true—he'd tossed that in at the last second and had no idea why.

"Works for me," Kerri agreed breezily, oblivious to his inner conflict.

He was silent, waiting for his moment. He pulled out his key and aimed it at his truck as if it were a flashlight guiding them in. Then he lunged ahead, opening the door. She smiled at him. Good. *Now.*

He glanced past the utility pole and, when he saw what was there by a park bench, the shock hit him as if one of the wires from overhead had fallen and hit him with a thousand volts. When he realized she might catch him staring, he yanked his eyes away.

"You okay?" Kerri asked curiously.

Not trusting himself to speak, Josh merely nodded. He shut her door and went around the truck and got in, his pulse hammering him. *It couldn't be. It just couldn't be.*

But, of course, it *was.*

They didn't talk much on the drive back to the shelter, though he could feel Kerri appraising him with her warm blue eyes as he concentrated on the road. He worked on keeping his face blank so she wouldn't see how upset he was. Gone was any consideration of asking Kerri for a date, or doing anything, really, except dropping her off and getting back to his dogs.

He was a little slow to get out to open her door and she managed it herself, sliding out with a quick smile.

"Thanks for lunch!" she repeated brightly, standing with the passenger door open.

Josh nodded a bit numbly, his heart still pounding.

"Right, then," she said, still smiling, though a flicker of something like doubt crossed through her eyes.

Josh waited until Kerri was back inside the shelter before turning the truck around and heading back to the parking lot. It was like scratching an itch you knew you shouldn't—he needed another look. He drove past slowly, gazing with sick despair. There. Standing by the bench, talking agitatedly with another man. Blond hair, scraggly beard.

Ryan.

Josh kept driving, past the clubhouse, up into the canyon, finally turning around when he realized there was no point continuing in the wrong direction. Ryan and the other man had left by the time Josh's truck cruised past again.

He was sick to his stomach as he drove home. "Hey, dogs!" he sang out with false gaiety when he walked in the front door. He could hear the puppies squeaking as he walked down the hallway to check on them, and Lucy thumped her tail, though they were feeding so she didn't get up.

"How you doing, Lucy? You okay?" Josh knelt next to her and ran his hand over her head and she gave him the smallest lick. The fur under her ears was so soft, he loved to stroke her there. "Such a good mommy, such a good, good dog, Lucy. Lucy, the good, good dog," Josh crooned. He felt better, holding her.

He watched her feed her little blind puppies for a few minutes, and it was as if he could feel that connection between mother and young, the flow of milk, of love, of life.

Why hadn't anyone ever told him about this, about having a dog? That it made every moment more important, that it somehow brought the best stuff to the surface of the day?

Josh sighed and stood. He went into his living room and looked through his window out at the thermometer, he went to the freezer to pull out a dinner, he emptied the trash— anything to avoid contemplating this new development.

Ryan was back. From France.

Now what?

NINE

The puppies' eyes weren't even open yet. They were helpless, virtually immobile, completely dependent on Lucy for sustenance. They needed their mommy. If Ryan came and got Lucy, the little puppies would die. From what little Josh knew of him, that sounded exactly like what Ryan would do, take Lucy away without thought of what it would mean to the babies.

That night the lights were on in the place next door— Josh could see them through the trees. In his own house, he turned off everything and sat with only the firelight, just like Lucy's first night.

I'm not home.

He waited all the next day for Ryan's knock on his door. Lucy picked up on his anxiety and followed him closely as he paced, practically stepping on his heels.

"Lucy," Josh murmured. "I don't know what to do."

After a second day of feeling under house arrest, Josh waited until dark and then slipped out the back door, shutting it in Lucy's face. He carefully walked through the woods, hating how much noise he was making in the silent trees, wincing every time he broke a twig underfoot.

His stealthy reconnaissance gleaned nothing of value.

Ryan's SUV wasn't in the driveway, but the garage door was closed. Some lights were on and a half-empty bottle of bourbon was on the counter. Ryan didn't step into view.

The next night Josh was back in the woods, and again, he didn't see Ryan. The suspense was like sleeping next to a rattlesnake, except Josh wasn't sleeping much.

"Should I go over there, Lucy? Get this over with?"

Lucy regarded him with nothing but support in her eyes.

"Okay, I'll go," Josh decided. "Just not today."

When Josh finally did go, he took a deep breath before he knocked on the front door. Ryan didn't answer. Peering in the window, Josh saw no sign of life. The bottle of bourbon was gone.

That night the lights were on, but still, no response when Josh rapped his knuckles on the door. Emboldened, he was there first thing in the morning, and again, no answer. Somehow Ryan's continued absence made him seem less of a threat. The knot in Josh's gut unclenched a little.

When the puppies opened their eyes, Josh felt as if he had a good excuse to call Kerri. But was it good enough? *The dogs have opened their eyes*, he would say. *Oh, and they all have blue eyes*, which must be pretty unusual, right? But then what? What if she waited for him to say more—there was nothing more to say! *They're squirming a lot more. How about that weather?*

You have the prettiest smile I have ever seen. Probably everyone told her that. Every guy, anyway.

That afternoon he brought Lucy with him to see if Ryan was there. It felt good to have a dog by his side until Lucy realized where they were going, and then she hung back, an unsure look in her eyes. She lowered her head and sat at the end of the driveway, refusing to accompany Josh any farther. "You're right, Lucy. We won't come here again," Josh told her. *Let Ryan come to us*, Josh decided. He was tired of living with the tension.

When Josh went online to research names for his puppies, he discovered that newborn dogs often have blue eyes when they manage to open them for their first milky look at the world. Calling Kerri to talk about that would have made him look foolish.

He spent two days deciding on names for the puppies, entering them into a spreadsheet that he printed and affixed to his refrigerator with the magnets that had Amanda's face imprinted on them.

NAME	GENDER	DESCRIPTION
Lola the Cuddle Dog	Female	Smallest dog, shortest ears, all brown and black. Needs to feed on two separate teats a day! Loves to cuddle, burrows into my arms when I hold her.
Oliver the Explorer	Male	Brown and white, brown face, white around mouth and stomach. Is always wandering off away from the others.
Sophie the Sports Dog	Female	Black, brown, and white with white tip at end of the tail. Fascinated with the toys in the pen, always sniffing them and moving them with her tiny little nose.
Cody Momma's Boy	Male	The only solid color dog; all brown. Doesn't seem to want to leave Lucy's side very much.
Rufus Loves Cody	Male	White face with brown spot over eye, brown and black body, white stomach, white tip at end of tail. Always sleeping with his head on Cody.

Except for Lola, whose ears were perky and short, all the dogs had ears that hung down, and all had snouts that stuck out like a Labrador's instead of being short like a boxer's. Their fur was short and their coloring a lot like a boxer's, with white, brown, and black predominant. Rufus was the silliest looking, with his white face and brown spot over his right eye. None of them looked anything like Lucy, who had the mostly black muzzle and alert ears of a German shepherd. But the vet and Kerri were right; if Lucy even noticed that her children were adopted, she didn't seem to mind.

Josh stood back and eyed his chart. He was aware that not a lot of people would take such great pleasure in organizing a bunch of dog names into a chart, but for him it caused the clean satisfaction of a job accomplished. His only dissatisfaction was that he really wasn't able to come up with much of a description for Rufus. Always sleeps near Cody? Yet Josh knew that if he'd left that square blank, it would have nagged at him and probably caused him to lose sleep. A spreadsheet needed things spread on the sheet.

Should he call Kerri to tell her he had named his dogs? That hardly seemed like a good excuse. Why hadn't he thought to get an e-mail address from her? E-mail would be easier than voice-to-voice. She'd pretty much put him on notice that she wasn't going to give him her cell number yet, so he couldn't text, but people were more free with their e-mail addresses, in Josh's experience.

Josh's text messages were routed automatically from his mostly dysfunctional cell phone to his PC, which was where he read a text from a colleague that told him, "Blascoe sez UI your FU," which meant that Blascoe was advising the other members of his former team that the problems with the interface were Josh's fault. Josh sighed in irritation when he read this—it meant he couldn't count on getting a good reference out of his most recent client, though maybe if he just told everyone that the project manager was Gordon Blascoe, prospective employers would understand why he got fired.

His résumé was out there in the job market right now—sending out inquiries was pretty much his sole occupation at the moment. This had long been his favorite part—launching his *curriculum vitae*, picturing them as little sailing ships headed toward the New World. He'd open the résumé and review it every morning, knowing somewhere out there people were reading it, people who would be impressed with his accomplishments. This time, though, the phone didn't ring immediately, the inbox didn't automatically fill with queries. Maybe it was a sign of leaner times, or maybe it was just the season—few IT departments initiated new projects in late October, when annual budgets were nearly depleted.

The danger now, Josh knew, was that his skills would atrophy or grow obsolete—in his world standing still meant falling behind. Josh signed up for some online courses and plunged himself into touch-screen application programming—phones, tablets, even ATMs. He made a master list for himself:

- Study
- Develop a demo app for smart phone
- Hike
- Call Kerri

Every day he consulted the list on his computer, but that last task somehow never got done.

He didn't feel good about leaving Lucy behind when he went hiking, but he didn't want to leave the babies without their mommy. Besides, his favorite route took him past the back of Ryan's place, and he knew Lucy wouldn't like that. Josh never saw any activity there, and he never went to the front of the home to see if there were any indication his neighbor was still around.

The puppies were not yet three weeks old when they began to exhibit a wanderlust. They weren't really good at walking—it was almost as if they were trying to swim in their box, propelling themselves on their stomachs or staggering around on wilting legs like little drunks. But whenever Lucy groaned and stood up to take a break from mommyhood, they would squeal loudly and then be on the move, trying to scale the sides of the box as if it were a prison break or working their way to the far end of the chamber to see if momma dog might be down there.

Already their personalities were asserting themselves—Oliver ranged the farthest and seemed the most frustrated to be walled in. Lola, the small female, would seek out Josh's voice, heading in his direction if she could find him, and would squeak in agitation until he picked her up—Lola just seemed to want to be hugged. Sophie wanted to paw at dog toys, while Cody and Rufus pretty much waited for Lucy to return, hanging together for moral support.

Lucy would often come to him and lay her head in his lap, as if to say, "I've had *enough*." Chunks of her hair had fallen out and she'd lost some weight, giving her a permanently exhausted appearance, and whether the air outside was chilly or warm and dry, she seemed to linger when Josh let her out to do her business, no longer in a rush to get back to her brood.

"Good dog, Lucy," Josh told her. Sometimes he'd kiss her on the face, and she'd lick him back. He loved to kiss her on the side of her muzzle, between her eye and her nose where there was a slight concavity. He couldn't tell if Lucy appreciated it, but she didn't bite him or anything, so he felt it probably meant she was okay with it.

When four days of clouds and cold wind gave him cabin fever, Josh put a box filled with the puppies on the floor of the truck's front seat and drove down into Denver to a chain pet store that allowed animals inside. He was thwarted, though, by a sign saying animals under eight weeks of age weren't allowed inside for health reasons. It made sense— the puppies hadn't yet gotten their shots. Josh left them in the truck and ran in to buy a few chew toys for Lucy. When he came back, three young women were clustered by the side of his vehicle, peering in at his puppies and making cooing sounds. He opened the door and let them hold his little babies, which seemed to cow Cody a little but Lola absolutely loved. Josh glowed with all the attention, especially when the women, saying good-bye, hugged *him*.

It struck him that maybe you didn't need Leigh and Wayne if you had a pickup truck full of puppies.

When he arrived home Lucy was watching from the window. Her accusatory expression seemed to say *I expected you home before now*. She needed to nurse as much as the puppies needed to eat, and Josh felt a little guilty when he saw how greedily the little ones went for Lucy's teats. As he had done every day since Kerri had given him the instruction, he made sure the tiniest dog, Lola, had a chance for two separate meals.

Lucy forgave him, though—that seemed to be what dogs did, they immediately canceled any grudges and excused any offense because it was just so much more fun to be friends. She jumped on a squeaky cow toy when he gave it to her, shaking it so that it gave off mad squeals that caused the puppies to nose each other in astonishment.

When the weather channel served up a miracle day— high seventies, no breeze, fluffy clouds—Josh decided to give the dogs a chance to romp. He lifted the puppies and put them into the same cardboard box and carried them onto the sparse lawn of his front yard. Lucy was anxious about the whole operation, pacing and yawning as if worried that Josh was going to head down to Denver again, but as soon as he gently let the puppies onto the warm grass she relaxed and went up on the front deck to take a snooze.

The puppies seemed pretty surprised to find themselves out in the open. They raised their wobbly heads to the wind, sniffing, and squealed at one another, none of them willing to leave the dog pile of siblings to venture farther into the yard.

Josh backed away to give them a dozen feet of freedom, lying down on his back with his fingers interlaced behind his neck, gazing up into the sky. What a day! It was easy, sprawling there, smelling the pine needles baking in the sun, to picture that it was the middle of summer on some long ago day. Maybe a Sunday—Mom would be making a roast in the oven and Dad would be reading the paper on the deck.

In a few days it would be Halloween, a complete non-holiday for Josh. No child had ever ventured up his long driveway to ring the bell in all the years he'd lived here. But for his mother, October was the time to get really serious about Christmas, which as far as she was concerned was a holiday that lasted six months. Decorations would start popping up overnight, like mountain flowers after a summer rain. Christmas cookies would fill the house with their warm, sweet scent as they baked in Mom's oven, and she owned VCR tapes of every Christmas movie a person could name, playing them ceaselessly both before and after December twenty-fifth.

Josh had them all on DVD now. Maybe he'd watch one tonight, like *It's a Wonderful Life.* Josh loved that one, how Jimmy Stewart comes to realize that nothing should ever change, and that the most important thing is to keep a family together.

Smiling in pure pleasure, Josh dozed for a moment, then

gave a start when he felt something wet nudge his arm. It was Oliver the Explorer, pressing his tiny black nose against him, the white around his mouth like the grease paint smile of a clown. Josh rolled and looked and the rest of the puppies were straggling behind their brother, all of them making their uncoordinated way to him in a ragged line.

Oliver put his small paws on Josh's side, trying to climb up on top of him. "Hey there, little guy," Josh murmured, pulling the puppy onto his stomach.

Soon little Lola was there, and then Rufus and Cody, with Sophie bringing up the rear. They all squeaked softly, trying to clamber on top of him, so Josh helped them and soon he had all five puppies up on his chest, a pile of little dogs, squirming and eventually falling asleep. That's how Josh spent the afternoon, his whole dog family on top of him, taking a nap.

That day seemed to be a turning point in the lives of the puppies. Now they wanted to roam, and would squeak shrilly until Josh helped them out of the box. They made little messes on the hardwood floor, which were easy enough to clean up, and otherwise just moved around, sniffing at the wall or jumping on each other in comically uncoordinated attacks. Josh kept the box in his sister's old room, which was a sterile place with a bed and a dresser reserved for guests he'd never had, and that's how their adventures always started, with Josh letting them out of the box and putting them on the floor in Janice's room. Oliver always ventured the farthest of all the puppies—soon, Josh knew, he'd want to be let outside. Lola always sought out Josh and wouldn't stop complaining until he picked her up. Sophie would find a toy to wrestle. Cody and Rufus usually were the slowest to emerge from the bedroom and were always together, inseparable.

It snowed on November first, the sort of teasing, dancing flakes that drifted around on the wind and seemed to be moving more sideways than down. Gradually some of the logs in the woodpile accumulated a little of the white stuff, like grandmother's lace laid delicately on the arm of a chair.

The phone rang while Josh was singing to the puppies. He ran to answer it, his socks sliding on the floor. It was Kerri.

"You sure lost interest in me in a hurry," she observed.

"What?" Josh gripped the phone. "*No*. I mean . . ."

She let him dangle at the end of his sentence a little while. "You didn't call me because . . ." she finally prompted.

"I don't know. There wasn't anything going on or anything," Josh replied. "Did you . . . did you want me to call?"

"Only if you wanted to call me."

He had no answer to that one.

"I came by to see you, but only Lucy was home," she continued breezily.

"You came by to see me," Josh repeated stupidly, his heart pounding.

"To see the puppies," she agreed.

"Oh."

"Where were you, anyway?"

Josh told her about his trip with the puppies in the cab of

the truck, describing the attention they received from people but neglecting to mention that all of the people were females.

"That's good, you should keep doing that," Kerri encouraged. "We need to socialize them. Get them with people. Also, need to do the same with other dogs. I've got a four-month-old terrier mix we named Bob who is just a love dog, plays with everyone. I thought I'd bring him out."

Josh desperately wanted Kerri to come out, but the idea of some giant four-month-old canine playing with the puppies gave him pause. "Won't he hurt these little guys? They don't really run very well."

Kerri told him it would be fine so of course he agreed she could come out around lunchtime the next day. Then he went to his laptop and tried to search on "the most popular lunch for women" but all he came up with was recipes for dessert.

Amanda's favorite lunch was chicken Caesar salad with iced tea. Her second favorite was Chinese chicken salad. The deli department at the grocery store luckily had both, so he bought generous helpings of each. He picked up six different types of iced tea to go with them.

Bob turned out to be a fluffy gray-black dog with hair that covered his eyes. Lucy growled at him from the front window when Kerri opened the tailgate of her car, a deep-in-the-throat noise Josh had never heard the dog make. "It's okay, Lucy," he whispered, not sure.

Kerri was wearing a sweater, tight jeans, and high boots. She shook her long brown hair exactly the same way as the very first time he'd seen her, and something like an electrical current buzzed through Josh's chest as he watched. She waved at him through the window while Bob sniffed at the bushes. Josh opened his front door.

"Lucy's growling," he called.

"Hello, it's good to see you, too," Kerri replied.

"Um, yeah . . . sorry, I'm just . . ." Josh felt like a complete idiot.

"She's just being a good protective mommy dog. Let her out."

Lucy was pressing up against his legs, eager to push out the door. Josh reluctantly stepped aside and Lucy ran out, her tail stiff and her ears erect, straight as a missile right at the intruder dog.

Bob reacted as if shot, falling to the ground, rolling onto his back, and wagging his tail. When Lucy bent over to disdainfully sniff him up and down, Bob wriggled and licked her in the mouth. Finally Lucy turned away from him in disgust and went to greet Kerri.

"Hi, Lucy," Kerri said while Bob crawled around at Lucy's feet, head low in submission. "See what I mean?" Kerri called to Josh. "Total love dog."

He came down his steps, his hands jammed in his pockets, and only realized at the last second that she was offering her cheek for a kiss. He managed to land his lips somewhere between her jaw and her ear. Her perfume wafted delicately on the air and he had to restrain himself from closing his eyes and breathing it in.

With Lucy back in the house and watching motionless from the window, Bob wallowed with the puppies, who swarmed him, nipping and squeaking. "They look more like Lab puppies every day except for the coloring. And what's up with Lola's ears? That's like Chow or Akita or something," Kerri speculated.

Every time Bob rolled on a puppy, Josh lurched forward, and every time Kerri put a hand on his arm to stop him. "They're fine," she assured him more than once. Soon that whole side of his body was warm from her touch. He could have been accused of maybe making a false move or two just to have her physically restrain him.

When the puppies were tired, Kerri and Josh carried them inside. Lucy went back to the box to feed them and Bob flopped on the floor and fell instantly asleep.

Kerri clapped her hands in delight when she saw the two big bowls of salad and the six separate bottles of tea. "You are hilarious," she told him. Josh loved that she was laughing but wasn't sure that the joke wasn't based on him being a fool. In his opinion, foolishness was not his chief attraction.

"You have tongs, maybe, for the humongous salads?" she asked. "No, I'll get them," she offered as he started to leap to his feet. "I'm closer."

"Drawer there, under the toaster," he said. He liked the look of it, Kerri moving across his kitchen like she belonged here. She opened the drawer where he kept things that defied category, like a hammer, a wine opener, tongs, crab crackers.

"Oh, hey," Kerri said. "While I was out here the other day?"

"Yeah?"

"I ran into your next-door neighbor."

"Oh," was all Josh could think to say.

Ryan.

TEN

S o, my next-door neighbor?" Josh prodded when he could speak. Kerri was pushing utensils around, distracted.

"Nice guy," Kerri remarked absently.

"Really?"

Kerri looked up at his tone. "What? Not nice?"

"No, he's fine." Josh cleared his throat. "What'd you two talk about?"

"Not much, really. Found the tongs," Kerri proclaimed.

Josh swallowed. "That's good," he told her in barely audible tones.

She sat at the table and cocked her head at him. "What's wrong?"

This was one time he did not want her reading his mind. "Nothing," he answered, shaking his head.

"He just said the former tenant skipped out on his rent."

It took a second to register. "Oh, my neighbor. James Hatch."

"Yes, that's right."

"Really nice guy," Josh babbled. "His daughter used to babysit us. He was an engineer, the kind that drives a train. Maybe a conductor, I don't know the difference. Anyway, he retired and became a fly-fishing guide. They used to live there but now he is down in Denver but he still rents the place."

"All good to know," Kerri observed cheerfully.

Josh felt his face go red. "Nice guy," he repeated lamely.

"Right, then let's eat lots and lots of salad."

They crunched their way through a few bites of salad. Why had he gotten something that made it so difficult to talk? He should have bought soup or pudding or something.

Lucy came out of the back bedroom, her nails clicking on the hardwood floor. She went to Kerri to be petted and then to Josh, where she put her head in his lap. He stroked her ears. "I know, it's hard," he told her. "They just eat and eat."

"You know? Experience in these matters?" Kerri teased, raising an eyebrow.

"I know it *looks* hard," Josh amended.

"You start them on solid food yet?"

"A little. Mostly, they just step in it."

Lucy went over to sniff at Bob, who thumped his tail and rolled on his back in utter submission. Then she turned in circles on her pillow and sank down into a nap with a sigh.

"I can bring a cat out next week," Kerri informed him.

"A cat?" Josh replied, his stomach doing a little flip over the notion that she would be coming back next week.

"We've got this tom named Waldo, he breaks in all the puppies at the shelter who need to learn how to behave around cats. And we need to socialize the puppies with children. Do you know any kids?"

"Well, yeah, who doesn't know some kids, of course I know some," Josh replied, thinking he must.

"I've got two in my building I babysit for sometimes."

He instantly decided that having her come out with children was a much better plan. "That would probably be a good idea," Josh agreed. "I don't know that many kids. I mean, I used to, back when I was . . . in school." *God, what an idiot.*

"Right," Kerri agreed tolerantly. She smiled at him, oblivious to what that smile did to his insides, which felt as if they were falling from a great height.

"So what have you been up to, besides being puppy master?" she inquired.

"Oh. Well, I like to hike in the mornings."

"I *love* hiking," she interrupted. "I used to drive up from Denver on the weekends but now, living up here, I can just head out anytime I want."

His heart gave a skip. He pictured her on the trail with him some afternoon. Soon, some afternoon soon.

"And then I'm taking some online courses in building applications for mobile devices and other touch screens," he finished. He flushed, realizing he sounded like a complete geek, but she just munched salad, looking mildly approving.

Puppy squeals suddenly chorused from the back room. Lucy opened her eyes but otherwise didn't move. "Sounds like the little ones just figured out Mommy isn't there," Josh noted. He set down his napkin and stood up.

"Probably best to just let them cry it out," Kerri observed.

"No, I can get them back to sleep," Josh replied. "Want to see?"

Curious, she followed him down the hallway.

The puppies were gathered at the near edge of the box. Rufus, his little brown spot like an eye patch, gave a tiny yip—the first bark any of them had made. Sophie had white paws which she pressed to the side of the box and a white tip at the end of her tiny puppy tail, which she started wagging when she saw Josh. Their squealing was even louder.

"Hey . . . Hey . . . let's give Mommy a rest," Josh murmured. He got down on his hands and knees and Kerri followed suit, right beside him. "Go to sleep, little puppies. Night-night."

"I don't think they're buying it," she commented.

"Just wait," Josh advised. "I've done this before. Okay? Ready?" And then he began to sing to the tune "Away in the Manger":

Away in a dog box,
A quilt for their bed,
The little dog puppies
Lay down their sweet heads

One by one the puppies stopped squealing and complaining. Lola, the smallest dog, lay down, and Oliver, his mouth painted white, collapsed more or less on top of her. The rest of the family toppled over as if anesthetized, sniffing and squirming before closing their eyes.

Lucy your mommy
Is just down the hall
But she cannot sleep
If you start to squall
So sleep, little puppies
Together as one
And when you all wake up
We'll have puppy fun.

The puppies were all asleep, Cody and Rufus in a tight knot by themselves and all the other ones in a heap with one another. Josh and Kerri were still on their hands and knees.

"I made up the lyrics," Josh murmured unnecessarily.

"Wow, that's the most adorable thing I've ever seen," Kerri whispered. Josh looked at her and it was so, so easy to just stretch his neck a little and meet her willing lips, that he found himself doing just that, with no thought or planning whatsoever.

Her perfume enveloped him and this time he did close his eyes, drinking in not just her scent but the soft, warm sensation of her mouth, which spread a glorious joy through his whole body. He knew in that instant that he would never forget this moment.

The kiss grew a little more enthusiastic, an idea seeming to occur to both of them at the same time, and then Kerri pulled away. "Look, wait. Sorry, but this is not happening here. Not in the Amanda museum."

Josh hid his disappointment as Kerri stood. He climbed to his feet and followed her back down the hall to the kitchen, uncomfortably conscious of the pictures of Amanda lining the walls. "Ready to go, Bob?" Kerri called.

"Don't you want some more salad?" Josh asked.

"No thanks, I only eat one tropical rain forest a day." She tossed a dazzling smile at him.

"Then . . . would you like to take some with you?"

"Right, sure. No more than ten or twenty pounds, though."

Josh wasn't sure what was going on. She was joking with him and grinning at him, but she'd just broken off what had seemed like a very promising first kiss. Did she like him or not? He put most of the salads into containers and handed them to her.

"Thanks. Come on, Bob," she commanded.

Lucy and Bob both jumped to their feet and followed Kerri as she went out the door. Josh stood awkwardly as she put the salad in the backseat and then lifted the tailgate for Bob. She had a dog crate in the back of her car that looked as if it had been in a war, the plastic sides cracked and covered with duct tape. She saw him examining it.

"One of the volunteers at the shelter backed over it," Kerri explained in response to the question on his face. "Luckily there were no dogs inside."

Bob jumped up and into the crate and then watched as forlornly as a wrongfully convicted prisoner as Kerri fumbled to shut the barred door.

"Bob seems pretty sure he'd rather ride somewhere else," Josh observed.

"He doesn't bark or cry, though. One dog howled at me all the way from Goodland, Kansas." She slammed the tailgate and then turned and gave him her amazing smile. "Right, so, next week, like Thursday after work? Waldo and I will come out, give the puppies some cat time."

"Sure. It's a date," Josh confirmed. Except it wasn't. A date was when romance was a possibility.

For a second he'd been sure romance *was* a possibility, maybe even a certainty, but now it didn't seem so, not at all. He didn't understand her. Why couldn't she just tell him what was going on? He watched her drive off and then stood looking in the direction she'd gone until Lucy nosed his hand.

Do you know any kids? The question somehow stirred him, made him feel restless and even regretful. He found himself dialing his sister's number—it was just after four back in Portland.

"Hello?" she answered, something in her voice telling him she knew from caller ID who was calling.

"Hi, Janice."

"Josh, wow, how are you?"

They chatted, checking in with each other. Neither of them had spoken to either of their parents in several weeks and both of them agreed that was wrong. "I just get so busy, with the boys in football and choir," she explained, sighing.

Josh had no such excuse, so, he just said, "I know." Then he cleared his throat. "So, hey. I was wondering if maybe you'd like to come visit? I have these puppies."

"Puppies?"

Josh explained about Lucy and the box left in his truck. "That's an amazing story," she breathed, awed.

"I was thinking the boys would really like to see them."

"Oh, I'm sure they would," Janice agreed.

Josh could hear her resistance and applied more pressure. "You haven't ever been out. Since I bought the place, I mean."

"I know, I just . . ." Janice blew out some air. "Can I be honest? I really don't want to see the house where I grew up."

"What? Why? It has so many happy memories."

Janice gave a short, sad laugh. "Seriously? All I remember is Mom and Dad fighting."

"Well, sure, but otherwise, things were good, weren't they?"

"Wow," she marveled, "you're still doing it."

"Doing what?" Josh responded defensively.

"Still holding all the pieces together. Trying to make it all seem good when it's not. Trying to make it the way it never was."

Josh was silent.

"I didn't mean to hurt your feelings. I'm sorry, Josh. I know how hard it was for you. I just . . . forget I said it, okay?"

"Sure," Josh replied tonelessly.

"Look, tell you what. Why don't you come out here? You and Amanda, I mean. It's the holidays, we've got room. We'd love to see you."

"Oh. I guess I didn't tell you. Amanda and I broke up."

Josh glanced up at Amanda's picture on the hearth, her smile belying his words.

"No! Oh my God, I'm so sorry. When did this happen?"

"Like, um, April."

"April? Why didn't you tell me?"

"I don't know." *Because telling you makes it seem more real.*

"Does Mom know?"

"No. I don't think so." *Same reason.*

"Are you doing okay?"

"Yeah, I'm fine. It was friendly. We're still friends." *Except that we haven't spoken since.*

"I'm really sorry. What happened?"

Josh sighed and closed his eyes. This was why he didn't want to talk about it.

"There's this guy," he began haltingly.

"Oh, Josh, I'm so, so sorry," his sister murmured softly.

"Yeah."

"Then . . . why don't you come out by yourself? The boys would love to see you."

"See, that's sort of why I called, I mean, I can't leave the puppies."

"Of course. What am I thinking?"

They talked for a few minutes before Janice had to hang up, begging a busy schedule. They promised to talk again soon and it felt like they really meant it.

The Amanda museum.

He found a sturdy plastic crate and went around gathering

up her photographs. It was a little unfair to call it a *museum*—there weren't that many pictures, no more than fifteen or so. Twenty, tops. He put the crate on the floor of the closet in his parents' room.

The mantel seemed really bare when he was finished, so he decided it was time to break out the Christmas decorations, knowing his mother would approve. A miniature Christmas village soon came to life, tiny carolers standing in front of a small church, houses glowing with real lights, a cute Christmas train pulled up to the station. All of it lived among the wispy cotton snow that Josh arranged, in just the right way, so that the lights reflected off of it realistically.

What the heck. He put on the Christmas music and strung the lights over the fireplace, sipping the Good Earth spice tea his mother always had ready when the little village went up. He even brought the step stool over to the corner of the hearth, the one his little sister, Janice, needed to climb to get a good look at the display. It didn't seem right to have the village there without the stool nearby.

A few days later he drove into town to pick up some groceries. He took a route that led him past the animal shelter, but he didn't stop.

The Thanksgiving displays reminded him that the big day was practically here. He went to the freezer case and picked a turkey dinner that had mashed potatoes and gravy and a cranberry-apple dessert. It looked pretty good on the box.

He drove past the shelter on his way home.

Kerri came out the next day. Lucy woofed when Kerri's

tires crunched into his driveway. Josh looked out the window and there she was, wearing a blue coat with a red and white scarf. She reached into the backseat and pulled out a large gray cat. Lucy moaned, as if saying, *Oh, no, not a cat.*

Josh opened the door with one hand while holding Lucy's collar with the other. "Lucy's not happy," he advised. Then he remembered the last time she'd come out. "Oh, hi, Kerri. It's great to see you."

She laughed at him, squeezing into the house as he backed up, pulling Lucy with him. "It's great to see you, too. Lucy, this is Waldo."

Kerri lowered her arms and Waldo poured languidly out of them and onto the floor, regarding Lucy with an utterly unperturbed expression. Josh released the collar and Lucy stepped forward, her tail rigid, her ears up, the fur a ridge on her back. Waldo sniffed Lucy's nose in obvious disgust.

"Lucy's been around cats, you can tell."

Lucy was most interested in sniffing Waldo below the base of his tail, which the cat put up with for about five seconds before whipping his head around and hissing. Lucy jumped back in alarm, looking at Josh accusingly.

"What did I tell you, Waldo doesn't take crap from anybody," Kerri chuckled. "Can we put Lucy in a bedroom? I want the puppies to meet their first cat on their own."

Josh shut Lucy in his parents' bedroom. When he returned, Kerri was standing in the living room with her hands on her hips, pointedly glancing at the Christmas village on the mantel.

"I see you've been doing some redecorating," she observed.

"Huh? Oh." Josh flushed.

"I like it. What will you put up when you take down the Christmas decorations?"

"Oh, uh, I've got some wooden ducks, and this wooden welcome sign I made in grade school."

"I like that even better. Can't wait to see it." She smiled at him and he grinned back, a full-on, helpless grin that employed all of his face and maybe even some of his shoulder muscles.

"Let's let the puppies out," Kerri suggested. They went down the hall together. "Wow, they're getting so big!" she exclaimed. The puppies sent up a chorus of squeals when they saw her. She and Josh lifted them out onto the floor, and when they turned and walked back down the hall, the puppies followed in a flood, bumping into the walls and jumping on each other's backs. Josh and Kerri stood in the living room and watched as they came skittering around the corner.

And then, as one, they spotted the cat.

ELEVEN

For a moment it was as if all the puppies had come down with a case of rigor mortis.

They froze in utter shock, staring at Waldo with wide eyes. When they twitched out of their paralysis they bunched up, massing together where the hallway joined the living room. Waldo stood in the center of the room as if in charge of the whole area. Heads bobbing, sniffing at the air, the dogs seemed completely flummoxed as to their next move. Oliver, out in front of the pack as usual, finally lowered his head and crept into the living room, his little tail wagging furiously. Waldo regarded his approach with unwinking eyes, totally bored. The other puppies began to follow their brother.

Waldo took two cat steps forward and that's all it took for the puppies to scramble back in absolute panic. They skittered down the hallway, virtually running over poor Cody, who had apparently not understood what was going on. Waldo settled at the near end of the hallway, blocking access to the living room, and stared coldly at the puppies, who were agitatedly milling around at the far end, jerking their heads up and down, wagging their tails, and crashing into each other. They instinctively hugged one wall, piling up like a traffic accident.

Kerri started giggling. Josh glanced at her and felt his heart go into mild fibrillation over that smile.

Oliver, still wagging his tail, decided there had been some sort of misunderstanding between himself and this strange, not-a-dog creature. There was no reason why they couldn't be friends, right? He stepped forward and his sisters Sophie and little Lola were right on his heels to lend moral support, albeit from a safe distance. He play bowed. *So far so good!* He took another few steps and bowed again. Waldo was still as a statue. The other puppies decided it was all going to turn out well after all and surged forward, Rufus stepping on Sophie's head in the process.

Waldo hissed.

Oliver threw himself into reverse, his eyes huge, colliding with the rest of his siblings in his mad dash to the rear. The puppies retreated en masse in wild terror. Halfway down the hall they skidded to a halt and regrouped in an anxious huddle.

"Something tells me we don't have to worry about them hurting Waldo," Josh noted dryly. What he really wanted, of course, was reassurance Waldo wouldn't hurt *them*. Kerri wasn't worried, though, so he tried to take comfort from her confidence.

Cody seemed to be getting bored—sniffing the walls, he was headed away from the action, back to the bedroom with their box in it. Rufus actually barked at him, as if saying, "Cody, get back here!" Cody ignored him.

Okay, new approach. Apparently elected ambassador because she was the smallest, Lola inched forward, her belly on the floor. Sophie, wagging her little tail like crazy, followed. Oliver, excited to see other dogs risking their lives, climbed on top of Rufus to get a better view.

Waldo observed the puppy delegation with a look of utter disinterest. The two girl puppies sniffed each other for reassurance, Waldo watching, unblinking. Encouraged by the lack of hostility, the puppies crawled forward on their stomachs like marine recruits going under barbed wire. Rufus and Oliver decided it must be safe after all and brought up the rear.

Waldo drew his lips back and that's all it took; the puppies fled as if running from a fire.

"Lesson one: kitties have teeth," Kerri pronounced dryly.

"Lucy doesn't seem to want to nurse anymore. She gets up in the middle of it and walks away, and sometimes she cries," Josh said.

Kerri nodded, absorbing this.

The puppies had reached the consensus that there was no cat. They were now trying to sneak past Waldo and into the living room by inching along the wall, deliberately not looking at the feline. Waldo's tail twitched. *No cat. No cat.*

Waldo suddenly sprang forward, leaping right up to the puppies, and they broke formation and tore down the hall all the way to the back bedroom. *Oh my God, there was a cat!*

Satisfied with a job well done, Waldo licked his paw.

"How are you coming with the solid food?" Kerri asked.

"I put the food out and they're eating it, but they still want to nurse," Josh replied. "I let them suck it off my fingers like you said to do."

"Usually the mom decides when nursing's over. Don't freak out if Lucy growls at them."

Josh frowned. "Freak out."

"What?"

"I'm not going to freak *out*."

"No, I . . ." Kerri laughed. "Sorry, I'm just remembering when you thought Lucy was going to kill the puppies because they weren't hers."

"Sure, but in my defense, I didn't have Internet to look it up."

"Your defense, so we're in court now? Am I the judge?" Kerri's eyes sparkled at him.

She was so beautiful at that moment that Josh found himself holding his breath. He wondered if the dismantling of the Amanda museum meant he could start kissing Kerri at will, because that seemed like a really good idea.

She was smiling at him as if she knew exactly what was on his mind, holding his eyes for a moment. "So anyway, they'll be weaned soon," she continued, filling the pause. "We like to wait until they're eight weeks to adopt them out, which sort of puts us in the middle of the holiday so we'll wait until after Thanksgiving. We'll put them on the website a few days before then, anyway. Puppies go pretty fast, especially cute guys like these."

Josh looked down the hallway where the puppies were assembled in the doorway as if seeking permission to come out. He decided that even if the puppies were weaned, they still needed their mother. And, just like that, he decided that he needed her, too. When and if Ryan showed up, he would fight him in court if he had to. He wasn't giving up his dog to anyone. "Can we let Lucy out now?"

"Why don't we shut the puppies in the back bedroom first?" Kerri suggested. "I don't know how Mommy would react if she caught Waldo terrorizing the babies."

They stepped around Waldo and went down the hall for the puppies. Cody and Rufus were off playing somewhere in the bedroom. *There is no cat.* Josh scooped up Oliver, who wriggled with joy, wagging and licking the air. "Where are your brothers, Oliver?" Josh asked the little dog.

"So, what are your plans for Thanksgiving?" Kerri asked as she hoisted the two girls off the floor. Lola wagged in pleasure, and Sophie's ears drooped—Kerri gave Sophie a kiss on the nose. "It's okay, little girl."

Josh was wrestling with her question. He didn't want to sound like some loser. What was he going to say, that he was going to celebrate the holiday using a microwave and maybe a couple cans of beer? "I'm cooking," he replied, which wasn't a lie.

"Really? Thanksgiving dinner?"

"Yeah, it's not hard."

"I'm impressed."

He shrugged, enjoying that he was impressing her.

"Like for friends? Any family coming?"

"No family. I invited my sister but they can't make it this year."

"Oh, that's too bad. So you have room for one more?"

"Sorry?"

"Want me to come?"

His pulse accelerated. Josh swallowed. "Yeah, that's . . . yes."

"You sure?"

"No, of course, I was pretty much thinking I would ask you but you probably already had plans."

"Nothing I can't change, it was pretty casual. I'd like to meet your friends. Want me to bring my pumpkin pie?"

"Yes! I actually was wondering what I was going to do about making a pie." *Also everything else.*

What was he thinking?

Answer: he was thinking he'd get to see Kerri. He'd do whatever reckless thing he needed to do to accomplish that.

They placed the puppies in their box. Rufus trotted out of the closet to greet them, emerging from the half that wasn't blocked by the sliding door. "Little Rufus with the spot on your eye, where is Cody, the other little guy?" Kerri sang spontaneously as she lifted him into the air.

It was silly and tuneless and she charmed Josh with her utter lack of self-consciousness. "Cody?" he called.

There was a rustling sound in the closet. The sliding door rocked as the little dog apparently bumped into it. Why didn't Cody just come out of the open side like his brother, instead of assaulting the door that was closed? Kerri put Rufus into the box, her beautiful long hair sweeping forward, and the puppy's siblings rushed him and climbed on him as if he'd been missing for a month.

Cody barked, a sharp, frustrated little sound. Rufus put his paws on the side of the box and barked back.

Josh went to the closet and looked inside. Cody was sitting next to a box, facing the slatted sliding door. "Cody? What are you doing?"

Cody turned at the sound of his voice, then banged into the box as he made his way over to Josh, who reached down and picked him up.

"What is it?" Kerri asked as he came out holding Cody.

"It's weird." Josh peered closely at Cody's tiny little eyes, which were black against his brown face. He set the puppy down on the floor. "Call him."

"Cody! Come here, baby!" Kerri got down on her knees on the rug, clapping her hands. The puppies in their box squealed, trying to climb out to get to her, stepping on each other's heads in the process.

Cody took a few hesitant steps in Kerri's general direction, but not in a straight line. She reached her hand out, but Cody didn't react to it. Kerri leaned forward, waving her hand. "Cody?"

Cody, sniffing, touched his nose to her hand. Instantly he was wagging his tail, going down on his belly and licking her fingers.

"He can't see," Josh proclaimed.

"Oh, poor little guy," Kerri murmured. She swept Cody up into her arms. "We should get him to the vet to make sure, though. Maybe there's something that can be done."

"Okay, but there's no rule or anything, right? I mean, you can keep a dog even if he's blind."

"Right, no, of course. They're harder to place, but we'll find someone."

"Or I'll keep him," Josh volunteered spontaneously.

Kerri lifted her eyebrows.

"What?" Josh responded a little defensively.

"You've never had a dog before. Seems like having a sightless one would be a lot harder."

But I'll have you around to help, he almost said. "I'm sure I could manage."

"Let's talk about it after the vet. I mean, just so you know, I hate it when people get a dog on impulse. It's a huge commitment. One of the reasons there are so many homeless animals is that people buy a cute puppy and then when it gets to be big and too much to handle they just dump it."

"Okay, but I would never do that."

She smiled at him. "I know." She held him in place with that smile for a long moment, his pulse bounding around like the puppies reacting to the cat.

They let Lucy out of the bedroom and she came out with her fur raised, obviously well aware that Waldo had been distressing the puppies. The cat just looked at the big dog, totally unafraid. Eventually Lucy decided to be magnanimous and forgive the trespass, though she shot Josh a surly look, clearly understanding that he'd been complicit in the insulting intrusion.

He walked with Kerri to her car. She put Waldo in the collapsing crate and then gave him her best knee-weakening smile, so that he had to lean on the vehicle for support. He was wondering if it would be okay to kiss her now, since they were right there at her getaway vehicle, but she surprised him by stepping forward for a hug. He pressed his cheek against hers and briefly smelled her hair before they broke apart. "Thanksgiving," he finally managed to murmur.

"Oh," she corrected lightly, "I'll see you before then, I'm sure."

Yes!

"We've got a new Jack Russell named Radar who just runs and runs. I want to bring him out—he's about the same size as your puppies, though he's maybe two years old."

"Okay." So that was it, he was going to see her because of the dog socialization program, not because he was wearing his best sweater and pressed pants. She was smiling at him. "What?" he asked her.

"Oh, nothing." What was she thinking? What was he missing?

After she left, it was a nice enough day for the puppies to play outside, Josh decided. It wouldn't be too long before winter socked the area with a big dump of snow and then the little guys would be confined to the indoors. He let Lucy out of the bedroom and picked up the puppies and carried them out to be with her.

"You're a good dog, Lucy," he told her. She gave him a cross look, still unhappy about the cat incident.

The phone rang and he dashed up the steps to get it. It was not, sorry to say, Kerri, but rather his buddy Wayne.

"Dude, I left you a voice mail," Wayne complained.

"Oh. You know that I don't really get cell up here."

"Can't believe such a high tech guy and you're still using a landline like it's nineteen-sixty."

"Maybe if you told me what your message was about," Josh suggested.

"Look, I know what you're going to say, but Leigh's got this friend from her yoga class."

"No."

"Dude."

Lucy started barking, barking in a way Josh had never heard before—there was something like anger in it, a ferocious growl. Wayne was still talking, but Josh was staring at the open door, not listening.

"Hang . . . hang on," Josh interrupted. He dropped the phone and went to the front window.

He gasped in horror when he saw why Lucy was barking. The dogs were under attack.

Canis latrans.

Coyotes.

TWELVE

It took Josh only a moment to take in the entire scene as it was unfolding.

There were two of them, young, lean, and hungry, hunting the puppies together. God, they were cunning. One of them was on the left, out of the trees, taunting Lucy, pacing back and forth just out of reach. Lucy was lunging toward this one, her face fierce, her lips drawn back, her shoulders hunched and her fur up. With every feint Lucy made, the predator would dance back, tantalizing, drawing Lucy farther and farther from her frightened brood, who were huddled together where Josh had left them. Lucy was drooling, her eyes wild, her teeth snapping.

The coyote who was goading Lucy with its taunts had an evil calculation in its eyes as it drew the dog forward, because the other hunter was in the tree line, circling stealthily to the right, waiting for Lucy to be lured just a few more feet before it darted out to steal a puppy.

Next to the door was the shotgun with the salt load. Josh grabbed it and racked in a shell as he ran out the door.

Lucy couldn't help herself. Enraged, she was charging the coyote on the left and the one on the right was making its move, darting out of the trees, mouth open in anticipation, ready to snatch a baby. "Hey!" Josh yelled. He leaped off his deck and stumbled. The coyote was almost to the puppies.

Josh fired a round into the air and the loud noise changed everything. The coyote on the right flinched, broke off its attack, and raced for the trees just as the other one fled from Lucy. Lucy went after it.

"Lucy! Come back!" Josh shouted, standing over the puppies. He racked in another shell. Coyotes were lurkers—they might appear to be in full retreat but they'd soon circle back for another look. "Lucy! Come!" Josh fired into the woods, the salt snapping at the trees.

Lucy came galloping back, panting. Josh doubted she'd caught up with the coyotes; they were consummate escape artists.

"Good dog, Lucy. Stay here," Josh told her. Lucy came to him, her wet nose touching his hand, the puppies squealing at their feet. Josh bent to them and that's when he noticed that there were only three.

Lola, Oliver, and Sophie were all swarming Lucy, seeking solace. Rufus and Cody were missing.

They were gone.

Josh gave into a heedless rage and plunged into the woods after the coyotes. He ran downhill, his vision clouded with fury and his face hot. He jacked in another shell, holding the gun across his chest like a charging soldier. He wanted to shoot the predators; he wanted to hurt them, beat them, kill them.

Fifty feet from the house he was in the thick of his lodge-pole pine forest, unable to run as fast because he literally needed to dodge trees. Looking down slope he could see well into the woods, though, and wasn't able to spot any sign of the coyotes or the missing puppies. He halted, panting.

Then he felt a shock of fear. What was he doing? This was exactly what the coyotes had been trying to do with Lucy; draw off the guardian and leave the family unprotected.

He turned and ran back uphill, his heart pounding, gasping for breath. When he burst out of the trees he saw that Lucy had Oliver in her mouth, carrying the puppy by the loose flap of skin behind his neck. Oliver looked cowed; his ears drooped and his little tail was curved up between his legs.

There was no sign of the other pups.

"Lucy! What happened?" Josh shouted in anguish. *No.* Had the coyotes returned and made off with Lola and Sophie, too?

The run back up the hill had exhausted Josh but he kept moving, up the steps and through the open door to his house. Lucy was just vanishing down the hallway and Josh pursued. The three puppies were all in the box; Lucy had taken them to the safest place she knew.

Josh shuddered to think about the puppies waiting out in the open, totally exposed, as Lucy carried them one at a time back into the house, but they were okay. Probably the gunshots had frightened the coyotes too much for them to circle back.

"You stay with the puppies, Lucy," Josh instructed her between pants. Oliver, Lola, and Sophie were all pressing anxiously against Lucy's side, maybe seeking solace as much as a meal. Josh shut the bedroom door.

He strode over to the gun rack and reloaded his shotgun, wishing he had something besides salt to shoot at the predators. Then he went back out into the front yard, stopping where the puppies had been huddled at Lucy's feet.

He couldn't believe he had done that—left the dogs out here by themselves, where besides coyotes there were foxes and even cougars, so that he could take Wayne's phone call. What had he been thinking?

He thought of little Rufus, the brown spot over his one eye, and Cody, blind and terrified, as the two little dogs were carried off by the vicious coyotes. The pain was almost more than he could bear. He sank to his knees, setting his gun aside, and put his hands to his face and choked out his grief in anguished sobs. It was his fault, all his fault. He was stupid, stupid, stupid.

He didn't track how long he wallowed in his agony. When he finally brought himself under control he wiped his wet hands on his pants. He knew something now. He wasn't going to give up the puppies for adoption—they were his dogs, and he would never abandon them again. It hurt too much to lose them. He just couldn't bear it.

He wondered what he was going to say to Kerri. Something told him she wasn't going to be happy with this choice.

But ultimately, Kerri would agree with his decision, wouldn't she? No, not easily. Josh knew she wouldn't accept it without argument, but he had to do it. He had to.

For some reason he found himself thinking of Amanda,

and a strong anger coursed through him. "It's no one's fault," she'd explained lamely as she packed her belongings into her car. As if the choice were made for her, as if her decisions were out of her hands.

Yes it is. It is someone's fault, it's your fault, Amanda.

Things were usually someone's fault. This, leaving the puppies to the coyotes, was his.

Just as quickly as it had come, the rage left, like a storm cloud that stabbed a single hot bolt of lightning at the ground before passing over the ridge and out of sight. His thoughts returned to Kerri, and he decided that for now, he wouldn't tell her anything about keeping the remaining puppies for himself.

Josh took in a deep breath, looking around at the yellow grass and sparse shrubbery that bordered his property. He'd have to build a pen for his dogs, one with a roof on it— mountain lions could leap over even a high fence.

When he heard the small squeak, Josh turned his head. It had been an animal sound, a little squeal. There it was again.

Josh's eyes widened. Could it be? He thought it had come from under his deck. Stooping down, he peered into the cramped, dark space, trying to see.

He spotted Rufus's tail first, the little white spot catching his eye and leading him to see the white face at the other end. "Hey!" Josh yelled, exultant. *They were alive!*

A man could crawl under there, and that's what he did next, his palms registering the rocky, cold ground. The puppies stiffened at his approach, Cody picking up on Rufus's agitation and sniffing frantically for a clue as to what this new threat was.

"Hey, Cody! Rufus! Come here, little guys." Josh gathered the dogs to his chest and wriggled his way back out. They weighed close to ten pounds apiece, now. Once he could stand back up he held them together up to his face and kissed them over and over. "Oh, you guys, I'm so glad you're okay!" he cried, dangerously close to tears. They seemed as intimidated as Oliver had been in Lucy's mouth, but Cody braved a little lick on Josh's nose.

When he opened the door to the back bedroom Lucy stood up and the puppies at her teats broke from her and fell away, squealing in protest. They immediately started lunging to reattach themselves, but Lucy stepped out of the box and went up to Josh to examine Rufus and Cody. She sniffed them up and down and they squirmed, their little tails wagging like crazy. The look she gave Josh seemed full of relief and gratitude.

Josh put the two wayward puppies in the box, but Lucy didn't seem to want to return. "I'll fix you some food," Josh promised the puppies. They started to squall as Josh headed into the kitchen, Lucy trotting at his heels. He petted the mommy dog and she licked his hand. Josh had a sense that there was a bond between them of shared adversity, of having been through something profound together.

The puppies attacked the soft food without any of their previous hesitation. It was as if, having survived a dangerous adult experience, they saw themselves as grown-up dogs now.

The phone was still dangling from its coiled wire, the

connection dead. He fed the puppies first, and then called Wayne back. Leigh, his wife, answered instead.

"Did you need to hang up so you could come up with excuses?" she demanded lightly.

"No, I had a thing happen. Did Wayne tell you I've got puppies?"

"Yes! Can we bring Isabella over to see them?"

"Yeah. I'd like that." *I do know some children.*

"Maybe we could get together after Thanksgiving."

"Um . . ."

"Or, I know! Do you have plans for Thanksgiving?"

"Actually—"

"It would be really fun if you came over."

"I was actually sort of—"

"There's someone I want you to meet. Thanksgiving would be perfect."

"Leigh—"

"I know what you're going to say, Josh, but come on," Leigh admonished. "You can't just sit around for the rest of your life, waiting for, for . . . I don't know. You need to *move on.* I hate how you do this, sometimes."

"What would it be like if I finished a sentence during this conversation?" His light tone belied his words—Leigh cared about him. It felt good.

There was a quick silence and then Leigh laughed. "Hey, sorry, it's just that Wayne said you weren't interested in Brooke."

"I don't know who Brooke *is.*"

"She's in my yoga class."

"What I am hoping to do by the end of this phone call is see if you and Wayne and Isabella want to come *here* for Thanksgiving."

Leigh was silent for a long beat. "Seriously?"

"Yeah. You're right, I *do* need to see other people, especially you guys, more often. My work sometimes leaves me isolated. And it makes more sense to come here because I don't even know how I'd get all these puppies over to your house."

"It's Thanksgiving. Who's going to cook?"

"Me."

"You."

"Yeah."

"You're going to cook."

"Come on, I don't see what the big deal is. It's just a dinner. I'll look it up."

"Oh my God."

"The pie's going to be good, anyway. A friend's bringing it."

"A *friend*?" Leigh replied, spearing the word like an owl on a field mouse. "Who? What's her name?"

Josh found himself grinning. "Kerri. So, what do you think?"

"Kerri. Where did you meet her?"

"I'll do everything, all you have to do is show up."

"From work? Who is she? How long have you been going out?"

"So probably this is where I tell you that if you want to meet Kerri, you need to come to Thanksgiving dinner."

"You do *not* tell me that! *Josh*."

They decided that Leigh and Wayne and their five-year-old, Isabella, would spend Thanksgiving at Josh's house. Josh had known that once he baited the hook with Kerri, it would be a done deal.

Look up how to cook Thanksgiving dinner, Josh typed into his task list.

The puppies were sleeping in a heap in the box, probably exhausted from their terrifying travail. Lucy didn't follow Josh down the hallway to check on them, just stood watching him with a *don't you dare wake up the kids* expression on her face.

Josh stood and gazed on his puppies for several minutes. Give them up? Impossible. They were his dogs. Nothing could change that.

When he walked back into the living room, Lucy stood holding a stout stick, almost a small log, in her mouth. She must have pulled it out of the kindling box. Her eyes were alert and merry, her ears up.

"You got a stick? A stick?" Josh asked.

Lucy stood rigid. When Josh cautiously approached, she moved her head, holding the stick away, but didn't try to run. What was he supposed to do, throw it so she could bring it back? Not in the house, surely. But this was the first time since he'd owned her that Lucy had wanted to play.

He grabbed the end of the stick and that's when he figured it out: Lucy set her paws and growled, pulling back. Josh put more strength into it and Lucy tugged back, firm yanks that nearly pulled Josh over.

They played tug-on-the-stick for about five minutes, and then Josh let go so Lucy could win. She lowered her head and dropped the stick on the floor as if daring Josh to come after it.

"You are so silly," Josh told her. Grinning, he went into the kitchen and Lucy followed, not protesting the end of the game. She was like that: willing to accept whatever happened, from being dumped on him by Ryan to having a box full of new babies thrust at her. They were a team—Josh felt as if, among all those he'd ever cared about in his life, Lucy was the only one he could rely on to stay by his side.

"You're my best friend, Lucy," Josh told her.

She sat with a *don't best friends deserve a treat?* expression on her face, and Josh gave her a small piece of cheese and some leftover chicken and some microwave bacon.

When the puppies woke up, Josh fed them and then tried an experiment. He pulled a rocking chair into the center of his living room, Lucy curled up on her pillow, watching him curiously. He tossed a blanket over the chair, tenting it so it was a large, shapeless mass. Then he went to the back room and picked up Rufus and Cody, who had been nuzzling each other in a corner of the box.

"Okay, let's see if I'm right," he told the little dogs. He set Rufus down first, then Cody, both of them on the kitchen side of the living room. Then Josh stood on the other side, near the big window. "Come, Lucy."

Lucy regarded him curiously. Clearly, in her opinion, nothing was happening that justified rousing her from her comfortable position. "Come on, Lucy!" Josh called, clapping his hands.

Lucy eased to her feet and went to Josh's side, her eyes saying, *There'd better be a point to all this.*

"Okay. Come on, puppies! Come on!" he called.

Rufus regarded him while Cody, agitated, began inching unsteadily toward Josh. Whether it was his calling or the smell of their mother that was drawing him, Josh didn't know, but he could see that Rufus didn't like the blanket-covered chair thing in their path. He eyed it, moving with Cody, who was blundering straight ahead while Josh continued to call.

As they got closer, Rufus turned into Cody, bumping him along the length of his body. The soft collision reset Cody's direction, and when it happened again the little dog was no longer on a collision course with the chair.

"Good dog, come on, Rufus! Cody!"

Cody slowed down, a little unsure until Rufus nudged him again. They were safely beyond the obstacle now, and they could both smell Lucy. "Such good doggies," Josh praised. When they got to their mother, they furiously beat their little tails. Lucy lowered her head and sniffed them.

Rufus had somehow decided to take responsibility for Cody, to steer his brother in the right direction when he was off course or headed toward something he shouldn't. That's why it had been the two of them under the front deck. That's why when Cody got lost in the closet, Rufus was in there with him.

"You are absolutely amazing, Rufus," Josh marveled, picking the little guy off the floor and kissing him on his brown spot. Rufus sniffed Josh's face, but seemed anxious to get back to Cody, so he picked up Rufus's brother and carried the two of them back to their box.

"Now," Josh declared with more confidence than he felt, "Thanksgiving dinner." He typed "Thanksgiving recipes" into his search engine.

He'd look up how to cook the turkey and all the other stuff.

What could go wrong?

THIRTEEN

Radar was a little white dog, ten pounds of flat-out energy. The puppies were all bigger than Radar, but they still ran with their uncoordinated gait, and thus stood no chance of catching him as he tore around in the front yard. The puppies tried, though, swarming in hapless pursuit. Every time Radar would cut a sharp corner the puppies would crash into each other, rolling on the ground, gamely leaping right back up.

Josh and Kerri stood in his front yard and watched this comical scene, laughing with pleasure. Kerri wore a gray woolen cap that set off her light blue eyes, and that smile of hers—Josh was laughing at the dogs but he was gazing at her smile.

"Poor Cody doesn't understand what's going on," Kerri lamented.

"Oh, he knows more than you might think. Plus he has Rufus," Josh replied, telling her about his experiment in the living room. They watched as the puppies, bumping into one another, cranked a tight circle on the heels of Radar. Rufus was on Cody's outside flank, turning him like a sheepdog.

"You're right!" Kerri stared at him in wonderment.

"The vet says a little light gets through to Cody, but not

much, not enough to really see anything. No idea why—Cody's just blind," Josh reported. "So Rufus is his eyes."

"Wow. I've never heard of a guide dog for a dog," Kerri marveled.

Radar smelled something interesting and abruptly stopped. The puppies helplessly piled into one another as the largest dogs, Oliver and Sophie, hit the brakes at the front of the pack. Radar let the puppies climb on him for a minute before streaking off again.

Lucy appeared at Josh's side, poking him with the stick in her mouth. Josh grabbed it and Lucy set her feet, tugging back. When she started growling, her puppies slowed in their pursuit, glancing over at their mother in alarm. But Radar darted back, enticing them, and the chase was on again.

When Josh let go of the stick, Lucy danced away, then immediately approached with it, waving it at him. Josh dropped to his knees and hugged her and she licked him, wagging her tail.

"You are so good with her," Kerri observed. Josh glanced up at her and there was that smile. He regretted that he was sprawled on the ground with his arms full of German shepherd instead of Kerri. "You're lucky you found each other."

"I know," Josh agreed.

Lola broke away from the dog game and went to Kerri to be cuddled, as if Josh's embrace of Lucy meant that it was official puppy-hugging time. Kerri held Lola cradled in her arms for a moment, then set the puppy down and pulled a small silver camera out of her pocket. "I want to get some pictures of the puppies for our website. We'll put them up now and say they'll be available for adoption after Thanksgiving."

Josh stood and dusted himself off.

"What's wrong?" Kerri asked, watching him. "Why that look?"

"Nothing."

"It'll be hard to say good-bye to the little guys," she speculated, reading his mind again.

"Yeah," Josh agreed. *Except I'm not doing that.*

He wasn't sure how Kerri would react when she found out that he'd essentially been lying to her about giving away his dogs. It wasn't something he liked to think about, but he needed to figure out a way to tell her. Tell her, without losing her.

Kerri had him lift each little puppy and pose it for the camera. Five separate times he buried his nose in puppy fur, smelling their puppy breath, feeling their rapid heartbeats through the palms of his hands.

"So, okay," he announced with finality as he set the last puppy in the photo session, Oliver, down on the ground. The puppy ran off to join the hunt for Radar, who was still circling tirelessly, wound up with his berserk energy. He took a breath. "Want to stay for dinner?" he invited, his voice as casual as he could force it to be despite the small tremors from his pounding heart.

"Oh," Kerri responded.

"We could stream a movie after, maybe," Josh continued, rushing it a little. "Or I've got all these holiday DVDs. *White Christmas, Miracle on 34th Street* . . ."

"I can't."

"Sure."

"No, I mean I'd like to but I have to go to Wyoming today."

"You have to go to Wyoming today," Josh repeated, looking for the part he was supposed to understand.

Kerri sighed. "It kind of came up last minute. See, in Denver, there's a law about pits, pit bulls—the breed is banned. It's ignorant, because they can be the sweetest and most gentle dogs, but that's it, there were a few attacks so now if your pit gets out and is picked up, they put it down. So the rescues there run sort of an underground railroad. We grab the pit bulls out of the system and hustle them out of the jurisdiction before they can be euthanized. A shelter up in Cheyenne has room for two dogs, so I'm headed up there in a couple of hours with these two pits and then I'm staying a few days with a girlfriend from college."

"Sounds like fun."

She was smiling at him. "Don't look so bummed. I'm coming for Thanksgiving, right? I'll see you then. Next week."

"Yeah. No, I'm fine, I think it's great, what you're doing." He kicked at the dirt. Why couldn't he seem to communicate what he needed to say to this woman? Why was he so, so . . . *stuck*?

As soon as Kerri left with Radar, the puppies shut down as if someone had thrown a switch. They collapsed in a pile, making it easy to scoop them into a blanket and drag the whole bundle down the wooden floor to their box. Josh didn't need to sing to them; they went to sleep unaided.

He walked back into his living room. The table was set with a linen table cloth, candles, and flowers. A small box of chocolates with a red ribbon sat next to where Kerri would have been sitting during dinner, near the ice bucket where he would have nestled the white wine after pouring them each a glass. The frozen chicken alfredo was in the microwave, ready to be heated, and the deli counter had prepared a salad and a fruit plate—nice small portions.

Josh eased himself into his chair and Lucy came over and put her head in his lap, her look saying, *Maybe next time.*

The day before Thanksgiving, Josh went out onto his property with the chainsaw and headed toward the stand of blue spruce his father had planted as a windbreak along the ridge that marked their property line. When he was a kid, his whole family would troop out for the Christmas tree selection, Janice and Josh always disagreeing on which one was most perfect. Now it was just Josh and his dog Lucy, who raced along the cold ground, nose down, snorting. When she looked back at him, her tail wagged as if she were saying, *See how much fun we can have if we just leave the kids at home every once in a while?*

It felt good to exert himself a little, his breath coming out as gusts of steam. The past several days had glazed the leaves with frost, the temperature not making it out of the teens. Still no real snow, this odd, dry winter—he hoped they'd have a white Christmas, but at this rate it didn't look good.

Oliver, frustrated he hadn't been allowed to go along on the adventure, was yipping at the big front window when Josh returned. None of the other puppies was visible—they were off in the back bedroom—but they came running when Josh opened the door. He put the tree where it always went and broke out his collection of bulbs and lights, which the puppies assumed he was doing for their benefit. Sophie wanted first dibs on everything in the boxes, and went dizzy staring at the bulbs all dangling out of her reach on the tree. They attacked the garlands and wanted to chew the lights. When he was finished, the tree looked ridiculous, everything crowded at the top so the puppies couldn't get at it.

Not for the first time, he stood regarding the finished product of the day's efforts and wished that all the old decorations and lights from when he was young were still available to him. They'd been lost somewhere during the time when Josh's dad had been renting the place. The new ones just weren't the same. He had a Santa standing by a chimney that only vaguely resembled the one that had so captivated his Christmas fantasies as a child. Next to the Santa was a larger snowman who moved his head and monotonously raised and lowered a mittened hand, accompanied by an oscillating mechanical hum. The old one made a different noise.

He fell asleep that night rehearsing his dinner plans in his mind. It was all mapped out. Turkey with real stuffing.

Banana bread. Baked potatoes. Kerri's pie. Wayne's wine. Canned peas. Canned corn. Canned pears.

Josh's mom always served her Thanksgiving feast around noon, as if eager to get it over with so that everyone could focus on Christmas. Josh consulted the Web and set a six o'clock arrival time. Wayne, Leigh, and their daughter, Isabella, pulled up first, and Josh went out to greet them.

Wayne stood up out of the driver's seat, grinned, and threw a football soaring over Josh's head. "Dude!" he shouted, which probably meant "Catch!" The ball bounced under the front deck, where Josh supposed it would remain for a thousand years.

Wayne raked his fingers through his thick blond hair, which ignored his hand-delivered direction to stay swept back and instead fell forward into his eyes, which it had been doing since high school. The sloppy haircut was emblematic of Wayne's life, which was disorganized yet attractive—for as long as they'd known each other, Wayne was getting his friends involved in some new business. Josh had, at various times, owned a piece of Wayne's restaurant and of his bottled water–delivery service and his mountain bike store. Somehow Wayne seemed to never be broke nor successful. On balance, Josh had probably made enough money on the sum total of all of his investments to pay for the turkey that was currently cooking in the oven.

Isabella was five years old and, when she grew up, planned to go into the princess business. Her hair was a lighter shade of her mother's blond, tied back in a red ribbon that matched her Dorothy-in-Oz sparkly shoes. Her eyes were the same startling green as her mother's, too—Josh had often speculated that some survival instinct had caused Isabella to reject her father's DNA in the womb.

Leigh's style tended toward the layered mountain-wear look—simple sweater, jeans, sensible shoes with rubber soles. Josh had never seen her wear much makeup but with those amazing eyes she didn't really need any.

"How's the job situation? You still broke?" Wayne asked cheerfully.

Leigh shook her head at him and then turned to Josh. "Is she here?" Her eyes darted past Josh and into the house. She was practically hugging herself with excitement.

Josh hugged and kissed her while Wayne picked their daughter up like a suitcase. "Not yet and stop it."

"Good. *Now* you can tell me all the details," Leigh urged eagerly, her grin wide with anticipation.

"What if there are no details? What if I just met her and that's it?" Josh asked.

"Impossible," Leigh replied. "There are always details."

Inside, the puppies reacted to Isabella as if she was a gift from the dog gods. Squealing, she sank to her knees as they climbed on top of her, pulling at the ribbon in her hair and jumping to lick her face. Her giggles made all the adults smile.

"Christmas tree up on Thanksgiving. As usual," Wayne pronounced. He turned to his wife. "Josh's family was the only one that had Christmas lights up the day after Labor Day, and left them up until when, Easter? Independence Day?"

Josh ignored him. "This is Lucy. Lucy, meet Leigh and Isabelle and their pet boy, Wayne."

Lucy approached Wayne a little warily, but was instantly comfortable with Leigh.

"I want this one, Daddy," Isabella announced, holding Lola.

"Told you," Wayne pointedly said to Leigh.

"This is going to be so much *fun*," Leigh predicted.

Josh shook his head. "Stop."

"Will she be here soon?"

"*Stop.*"

They all turned when a vehicle pulled in the driveway. Even the dogs looked up.

"That's her!" Leigh gushed.

"Leigh, quit smiling like that," Josh warned her. "Just look normal, okay?"

The first thing out of Kerri's car was a leg—she was wearing a red plaid skirt and a tight white sweater. Josh had to force himself not to gape at her through the big window. He met her at the door and took the pie from her. He introduced Leigh and Wayne, who were acting as if they'd decided to abandon adulthood and go straight back to junior high school.

"I am so glad to meet you!" Leigh sang, pulling Kerri into a hug.

"Well, hi, me, too," Kerri replied, laughing a little. Leigh's vibrant eyes were flashing with joy, and Wayne literally gave Josh a thumbs-up. Wincing, Josh pulled Kerri around the couch to where Isabella was sitting on the floor with the puppies.

"And this is Isabella. Isabella, this is Kerri."

Isabella gestured to Lola, who was lying placidly in her lap. "This is my puppy."

Kerri sat down next to Isabella and Leigh joined them, the puppies swarming them, overjoyed at the new arrivals.

"I'll get some wine or something," Josh muttered. Wayne followed him into the kitchen.

"Dude!" Wayne enthused.

"Stop."

"No. Seriously."

"No. Stop."

"She's really hot. Whoa."

"Can we talk about this sometime when she's not within earshot? And would you please tell Leigh to get that look off her face?"

"I can't make Leigh do anything. That's why I married her."

"You married her because she was the only female who would go out with you in a six-state area. Please, okay?"

"You *like* this one," Wayne computed. "Whoa."

"If you don't start acting like a normal person, I'm going to send you home with a puppy."

Leigh came into the kitchen, smiling widely. "Oh my God, she's fantastic," she whispered too loudly for Josh's taste.

"You make it sound like I picked out a nice sweater or something," Josh complained.

"A very nice sweater. Especially in front," Wayne volunteered.

"The way she looks at you? She adores you, Josh," Leigh beamed.

"Hi!" Kerri greeted, coming into the kitchen. They all turned and looked at her. She stopped, glancing between them.

"Yes, we were all talking about you," Josh told her.

Things loosened up a little after the wine was poured. Isabella decided the dogs needed a bath and Josh gave her a wet washcloth, amused that Lola and Oliver both sat still while she stroked them with it, singing softly to herself. He was surprised Oliver didn't grow impatient and go off exploring, but he knew Lola would endure anything for human attention. The other puppies decided a bath wasn't an approved Thanksgiving activity.

It was, Josh decided, going *perfectly*. Once Wayne and Leigh got over their little-kid-at-Christmas excitement about Kerri, they all felt very comfortable with one another. Josh kept an eye on his turkey and other dishes in the kitchen, but as he understood it nothing much happened until the timer went off. At one point he was standing in front of the open oven, delicious dinner smells wafting out on the heat wave, when Kerri came to join him.

"You're not supposed to open the door while something's cooking," Kerri said.

"You're not?" It hadn't said anything about that on the website.

"What a cute little girl. My God. Will their parents take a couple of dogs in trade?" Kerri asked.

"No, but we could probably get Leigh to take a piece of pie for Wayne."

It was a small, cozy kitchen. Kerri made it smaller and cozier by stepping close to him, smiling up at him. His arm went around her waist with no conscious effort.

"You really have no idea how handsome you are, do you?" Kerri whispered to him.

The phone rang, but for a moment they didn't react, just looked into each other's eyes. Then Josh's expression flickered as it occurred to him it might be Ryan.

"Want me to get that?" Kerri asked.

"Sure." Josh remembered the cold fury in Kerri's voice the day he'd called to see if the shelter would take the newborn puppies, the day she said he might as well kill them himself. Let Ryan have a discussion with *that*.

"May I tell him who's calling?" Kerri asked. Wayne wandered into the kitchen, snagging the wine bottle and refilling his glass.

"Smells good in here," Wayne rejoiced, his happiness reinforced by the wine.

"Just a second," Kerri told the phone. She held it out to Josh. "It's Amanda," she informed him, her face expressionless.

"Oh. Okay," Josh replied weakly. He glanced at Wayne, who was standing with a stricken look, absolutely no help at all.

"Hi," Josh said into the phone.

"I'm calling to wish you a happy Thanksgiving," Amanda greeted.

His stomach felt drop-kicked. Her voice was the same, deep and rich and sexy. He licked his lips. "Happy Thanksgiving," he croaked back.

"Who was that who answered?" she wanted to know.

"Who?"

"The woman. Who answered the phone?" There was a shrewdness in her voice.

"Oh." Josh spun in a circle, wrapping the coiled phone wire around himself. "That's nobody. Just a friend."

Amanda said something light in return but Josh didn't hear it; his head was filled with a roaring sound now, a panicked, plaintive inner wail because no matter how very much you might want to take something back, once it's uttered, it's out there forever.

"I didn't realize I'd be interrupting anything," Amanda was saying.

When he looked up, only Wayne stood with him in the kitchen. Josh's front door was still swinging on its hinges, and Kerri's brake lights flared an outraged red as she backed up and swung her car around.

There was nothing to do but stand there and watch her drive away.

FOURTEEN

It was entirely possible that Josh said something intelligent and appropriate to Amanda during their brief conversation. All he could remember afterward was telling her that Wayne and Leigh were there and calling Leigh to the phone while he and Wayne gazed at each other with doomed expressions. Leigh pierced Josh with an unforgiving stare before grabbing the phone and smiling while she chatted with Amanda, who was an old friend.

Josh went to the front door and shut it, the cold outside air coiling around his ankles.

"Whoa, dude," Wayne observed, combining his two most overused words into a grave proclamation. He shoved his hair out of his eyes and it flopped back.

"What happened?" Leigh demanded when she got off the phone. "What did you say?"

Josh shook his head. He sat on the floor next to Isabella and Lola climbed into his lap. Leigh turned her attention to her husband. "Wayne?"

Wayne acted as if he'd just been caught eating the last piece of pie, holding his hands out in ridiculous denial. "Hey, don't look at me."

"What's going on?"

"Let's just have Thanksgiving," Josh muttered. Lucy, acting as if she sensed his mood, came over to him and licked his face. Lola went wild in Josh's lap, trying to jump up to kiss her mommy.

"Was she angry that Amanda called? That seems a little overreacting to me," Leigh observed critically. "You did tell her *about* Amanda, right?"

"Of course."

"I mean, all about her. Your relationship and everything," Leigh elaborated.

"Sure, I—"

"Because women hate it when you hide things about your past."

Josh shook his head. "No, I didn't—"

"Especially ex-girlfriends," Leigh added.

"I'm not hiding anything!" Josh snapped, exasperated.

"Then what did you do?"

"He said that Kerri was nobody, just a friend," Wayne piped in. Josh shot him a look and Wayne held up his hands again. "Dude, she always gets it out of me anyway."

"You said that? Oh, Josh, why?" Leigh asked plaintively.

"I don't know, I just clutched. I haven't talked to Amanda since she moved in with that guy, and her voice just . . . I don't know."

Though nothing was mentioned about it on the website, it turned out that cooking the banana bread in the same oven as the turkey was a bad idea. "Banana soup," Wayne proclaimed. And Josh must have missed the instructions to poke holes in the potatoes before zapping them—he would have said microwave preparations were something of a specialty for him, but with what sounded like a small-arms fire going off, the potatoes violently killed themselves. The dressing looked, in Wayne's helpful words, "like used chewing tobacco," and the turkey, alas, flowed pink juices when Josh sliced it.

"At least the pie will be good." Josh sighed mournfully.

"Your oven doesn't feel hot enough to me," Leigh speculated. "At three-fifty, it should be really warm. How old is it?"

"I don't know. I mean, it was here when my parents bought the place," Josh replied. "It was my mom's."

"You say that like she's dead or something," Wayne observed.

Josh shrugged. "I just like having it."

"Dude, who holds on to memorial appliances just because your *mom* cooked on it?" Wayne jeered.

Leigh gave him a sharp glance and Wayne shut up.

By microwaving the turkey slices, mashing the exploding potatoes and adding butter, and serving the canned vegetables, Leigh turned the disaster around—though everyone agreed that the best part was Kerri's pie.

Isabella fell asleep on the couch, holding Lola to her chest. The other puppies were in a heap on Lucy's pillow, Sophie with a small rubber toy gripped slackly in her mouth. Lucy sat with Josh in the living room. He and Leigh were drinking coffee while Wayne did the dishes.

"You need to do the dishes because you didn't do anything else," Leigh had explained to him.

"Whoa, what? What do you mean?" Wayne had objected, apparently believing that standing around in the kitchen watching Josh ruin the holiday meal and chase off attractive women counted as a contribution. He meekly did what Leigh told him to do, though, because that was how their relationship worked.

"Do you know what kind of flowers she likes?" Leigh wanted to know.

"Who?"

"*Who?* What do you mean, 'who?' Kerri. Don't send roses, send, orchids, or white tulips. Roses are too romantic and you need to apologize for being such a jerk and not imply that you expect things to just take up where you left off or something."

"I'm not going to send flowers. I'd look like an idiot," Josh objected.

Leigh's eyes were full of pity. "You know, underneath, you're a great guy, right? You just . . . I wish you were more social, is all."

Josh busied himself arranging the wood fire. Lucy came alert when Josh picked up a new log to toss into the flames, then sat down with a sigh of disappointment when he didn't offer an opportunity to tug on it. Her puppies became semiconscious when she rejoined them on her pillow, rearranging themselves with quiet peeps.

"I'm probably ruining these dishes!" Wayne called from the kitchen. He banged a couple of pots together to demonstrate.

"You're doing fine, honey," Leigh assured him. She was

examining Josh when he sat back down next to her. "I need to tell you something," she advised. She read his look. "No, it's not about you screwing up with Kerri or anything like that. It's Amanda."

Josh watched her. "What?" he asked finally.

"She said she's not happy. With her new situation." Leigh shook her head. "I'm just worried how you're going to react. She didn't say she wanted you back or anything. You know what she's like, she doesn't really know what she wants. God, isn't that just like her to call out of the blue like that? Part of me really wishes that I never introduced you guys. It's just that, well, you know. You don't exactly get out there. I mean, I felt like I had to do *something*. But it turns out she's just really selfish. I didn't know that." Leigh's green eyes searched Josh's face. "Anyway, so, I wanted you to know. I'm not sure what she's going to do. But now you'll be prepared, in case she calls again, and Kerri's here. So you don't mess up again."

"I'm putting the wineglasses in the dishwasher!" Wayne warned.

"Hand wash them," Leigh called back, her eyes still on Josh.

Josh shrugged. "You mean *if* Kerri's here." He had a pretty sure sense that she wouldn't be.

"You guys are great together. I like her, Josh."

"Let me ask you. Did you know about Amanda and this guy? Before, I mean."

"Josh."

"Come on. Did she tell you?"

"I don't even know *now*, Josh. Amanda never told me anything. She wouldn't, she knows how much I care about you. Amanda and I are friends, but I *love* you."

"So you would have told me? If you'd known something?" he pressed.

Leigh searched his eyes. "Would you have *wanted* me to tell you?"

What a question.

"Dude, I almost dropped this glass bowl!" Wayne exclaimed.

"Good catch, honey," Leigh praised.

They were silent for a moment. Josh gazed sightlessly at Isabella and Lola asleep in a sprawl on his couch. "So," he said, clearing his throat. "Amanda's what, thinking of leaving him?"

"Josh. *Really?*"

He bit his lip, looking away. Leigh patted his knee. "Orchids. Tulips. Not roses."

Wayne managed to finish the kitchen without destroying anything, though he made several more dire pronouncements in the process. "Kitchen's done except the turkey, you want me to put it in the fridge or call a hazmat team?" he announced, coming out with a towel in his hands.

Josh said he'd take care of it. Wayne picked up Isabella and Josh picked up Lola and they were both equally unconscious, hanging loosely in their hands. He held Lola in his arms, waving in his window as he watched his friends drive away, feeling unaccountably sad.

The following Sunday he woke up thinking about everything Leigh had said. *Amanda's not happy with her new situation.* He went to the plastic box in his parents' closet and pulled out the picture of her he'd taken when he'd flown her to Kauai for her birthday. She had been happy with her situation then. They both had been happy.

I just wish you were more social. Underneath, you're a great guy. "Underneath," Josh muttered.

The puppies were squalling, so he went back to let them out. It was another weird winter day, frigid but so dry Josh's skin hurt to be out in the air. The dogs weren't really sure why he always took them out to the cold yard behind the house as soon as they woke up, not connecting the need to squat with the fact that they often seemed to be outdoors when they did it. Oliver usually bolted for the trees, wanting to conquer new worlds, and Sophie usually found a stick to add to her toy collection, though she never seemed upset when Josh gently pulled it from her mouth before letting her back inside.

The others just waited for Josh to give them some sort of clue as to what was going on. In fact, they all seemed to look to Josh to decide everything for them. If Lucy was their mommy, Josh was the daddy. They ran to him when he knelt, they craved the touch of his hand. He loved picking them up and kissing them on their little noses. He'd never really thought about it before, but there it was: when you had dogs, they loved *you.* They never even thought to look for a "new situation." They never said you were a "man-child" obsessed with the past, acting like it was somehow your fault that they met some guy at work and decided the new situation would be living with him in Fort Collins.

Lucy played with the puppies, rolling them with her snout, but rebuffing any attempts they made at accessing her teats, which looked to Josh as if they were rapidly receding. Josh laughed at how the dogs tumbled, and shook his head in amazement at how adroitly Rufus steered Cody back to the crowd when the little guy strayed too far away.

This was it, this was the thing he could cling to: the happiness he felt with his dog family. Amanda haunted him like a ghost and he'd blown every opportunity he'd had with Kerri, but everything was okay when he was watching the dogs.

I just wish you were more social. Leigh was right; he needed to get out of his rut.

Down the hill was a small pond where the neighborhood children skated in the winter and, if they were very young and optimistic, fished in the summer. Josh put the puppies in a wooden crate, loaded them and Lucy in the front of his truck, and drove down there to see if there were any kids around who might want to see the puppies.

It was a blindingly clear day. Josh parked next to two vehicles that had pulled off the road by the frozen pond, changing his plans when he considered how the adults might react if he approached the children and told them he had puppies in his truck. He grabbed the crate and, marveling over how heavy the puppies had gotten, headed down to where the children were sliding around on the ice. Only one of the half-dozen kids had skates—a little girl in full Olympic figure skating dress who frowned in concentration in the center of the pond, trying to twirl. Two men sat on a crude wooden bench, talking to each other while a handful of boys kicked a plastic disc around on the ice in a game somewhere between soccer and hockey. Huffing with exertion, Josh walked over to the men with his container of puppies. Lucy was a little anxious, jumping up to look in the crate, where her brood was unsteadily riding out the movements and climbing on top of each other to try to catch a glimpse of where they were going.

The men regarded Josh's approach speculatively. "I've got some puppies, here," Josh greeted awkwardly. "I was thinking maybe the kids might like to see them. You need to socialize dogs when they're young, get them used to people."

The men stood and peered into the wooden box. They were both taller and heavier than Josh, both with dark hair and plaid shirts under drab jackets. Josh wondered if they were brothers.

"Fine with us," one of them grunted after the two men passed a glance between them.

"Hey, want to see some puppies?" Josh called to the children. The boys abandoned their game and rushed over. They looked to range in age from eight to ten, maybe, all with noses red from the cold. They clung together and slid to a stop in front of Josh.

"Look!" one of the boys cried.

Inspired, Josh went out on the ice and set the crate down with a thump, tipping it up on its side. The puppies came out in a jumble.

"Can we pick them up?" one boy asked.

"Just be careful," Josh agreed.

One of the boys went down on his knees and Sophie grabbed his scarf—toy!—in her tiny teeth and pulled it off him. Immediately she tried to run away, her feet sliding out from under her, with Oliver in pursuit. They couldn't get traction; when Sophie tried to change direction she fell, and when Oliver grabbed at the scarf his momentum spun him in a circle.

The girl glided over. "Be careful with your skates, sweetie," Josh told her. She solved the problem by sliding down on her hands and knees, reaching for Lola and gathering the little dog to her chest like an infant.

The dads on the bench decided they couldn't resist and came over to play with the dogs. Josh threw the plastic disc for Lucy, who ran like a cartoon character, her legs scrabbling underneath her unproductively and then, when they seized enough purchase, propelling her right past the disc while she dug her claws in, her legs spread apart. Sophie ran over, too, but wasn't quick enough to deprive the mommy dog of her prize.

The boys eventually came up with a game where they ran in circles on the pond, hanging on to each other, while the puppies slid and spun in pursuit. The little girl changed out of her skates to participate, giggling and laughing with the rest of them.

"Kind of dogs are they?" one of the dads asked. "Beagle mix?"

"Nobody knows. Maybe Lab/boxer/Akita. Abandoned at birth so we'll never know unless we do a DNA test," Josh explained.

"They for sale?"

"Oh," Josh responded. "Uh, no, they're just my puppies."

The man looked at him oddly, but didn't say anything.

When the puppies were slow to untie themselves from a particularly spectacular pile-up, Josh figured they were getting tired and it was time to head home. The children pleaded for five more minutes and he granted their wish—they weren't his kids; it wasn't his job to teach them the perils of instant gratification.

Josh sang "Jingle Bells" to the puppies in the front seat of his truck and they were all sound asleep when he arrived home. He swung into his parking spot, a bit surprised at who he saw sitting in her vehicle in his driveway, her engine running to keep her heat on.

Kerri.

FIFTEEN

Josh opened his door and Lucy bounded across his lap and trotted over to where Kerri was standing up out of her car. They greeted each other, and then Lucy went off to explore the yard. Josh got out of his truck, leaving the puppies in a sleeping sprawl in their crate on the floor.

"Hi," Josh greeted cautiously, blowing the word out in a cloud of steam.

"Look, Josh. I'm sorry. I totally overreacted. That was so rude and so, so . . . I don't know why, why I did that," Kerri apologized. "I needed to tell you that in person."

Josh took a step forward. "Okay," he said agreeably, but when he took another step toward her, she backed up a pace.

"Nothing you've done, we've done, suggests any kind of thing with us," she continued, brutally matter-of-fact.

"Kerri . . ."

"Anyway. Thanks for the flowers but you didn't do anything wrong. I was the one who was out of line." Her eyes didn't back up what she was saying; they looked wounded and more than a little angry.

"It's just that it's the first time that Amanda's called since she left," Josh started to explain.

"Oh, let's *not* talk about Amanda, okay?"

Josh looked at her, searching for softness he couldn't find. There didn't seem to be any right thing to do.

"Anyway," Kerri said.

"Want to come in?"

"No. I just came out to apologize. Oh, and good news."

"Good news," Josh repeated.

"We got applications for the puppies—like, a lot—and have approved a couple of them. It really helps because when people register on our website we can let them know about other dogs, even if they thought they only wanted a puppy. So, today's Sunday. How about Wednesday, want to bring them down then?" She gave him a probing look. "What is it, Josh?"

How did she do that? He thought he was wearing a perfectly neutral expression but she could see that something was troubling him.

"I need to get the puppies inside," he replied evasively. "Going to get cold in the truck, soon."

She followed him into his house, but waited in the living room while he took the puppies back to bed. Lucy curled up on her pillow by the fireplace. Kerri had her arms folded when he returned.

"Want some coffee or something?" he stalled.

"What is it you don't want to tell me?"

Josh looked at the carpet. "I'm not doing it."

"Sorry?"

"I'm not giving up my puppies."

"Oh," Kerri murmured after a moment. Her voice carried some pity in it, so he looked at her, a bit gratified to see that the stony look on her face had softened. "I know it's hard. But you can't foster failure a whole litter of puppies. It's not even legal."

"Failure?"

"Foster failure, it's what we call it when someone temporarily takes care of a dog and it turns permanent."

"You say failure, but actually it's a good thing."

"Perhaps, but not when it's six dogs."

"Six?"

"I'm counting Lucy."

"Oh. Right." For some reason it hadn't occurred to him to include Lucy in the count.

Kerri sat down in Josh's big chair, unbuttoning her coat and shrugging it off. Josh did the same on the couch, forcing himself not to reveal how happy her gesture had made him, how relieved he was over the implication that she wasn't immediately bolting from his house.

"I get how hard it must be," she said sympathetically.

He didn't like that very much. That's what people had told him when his mother had so abruptly moved out, and ultimately Josh had concluded they knew *nothing* about how hard it must be.

"You've never had a dog before, so you've never gone through any of it," Kerri continued.

"Okay, so we've established why I don't know anything."

She blinked at his tone. "I didn't mean that, Josh. I was actually talking about saying good-bye to them. Because when you adopt a pet you know you're headed for heartbreak, you know? Dogs are with us for such a short period of time. They are our best friends but we only have a decade, maybe a decade and a half, and then they're gone. That's what I meant. So losing them is just part of the deal, something you have to learn how to cope with. But listen, I really, really believe that one of the lessons they teach us by loving us so intensely while they *are* here is that we need to celebrate life while we have it, that yes, everything ends and we have to move on but that while we're here we should make sure we don't waste it, you know? I mean, my mom has been numb like half her life, what kind of existence is that?" Kerri's eyes were moist, and she wiped at them hastily. "And when we lose them, when they do die, I honestly believe that the last thought on their minds is that they hope we get another dog."

Kerri's face was red and she took several deep breaths. Josh knew this was somehow an important moment for them, that they were supposed to be sharing something, but he searched inside and all he felt was a cool remoteness. He couldn't get past the fact that she was essentially arguing he should give up the puppies.

"I don't understand what you're saying," Josh finally responded.

"I guess I'm just saying you can't keep them because, well, you *can't*. No one can, not for as long as we'd like to. So the thing to do is to understand that what dogs give us is always just a brief period of time of being with us, which has to be good enough because it's all there is. So we need to celebrate it while we can, and then move on. That's the lesson of the dogs, that it's important to both live in the moment and then go on to the next wonderful thing."

"Is this a speech you give to people? Like, foster dog parents, when they take in dogs but can't give them back?"

"Maybe a little," Kerri admitted with a small smile.

"It's pretty good."

"Thanks. Plus, I usually say that the main reason I work at the shelter is for the animals, but that there's something about the joy you can give people when you bring them together with their new dog. Animals are so confused at the shelter, and then they're so grateful when they are given a forever home. I want you to experience that."

"But that's not what happened, here. I didn't volunteer for this. The puppies were put in a box in my truck," he argued.

"Right, but Josh, six dogs? Come on. One puppy is a lot of work; I can't even imagine what it would be like with a whole litter. Isn't it enough that you'll have Lucy?"

"No," he said shortly. Lucy looked up at her name, then set her head back down, intently watching Josh. It was as if the dog knew what was going on inside him.

"Then keep one. Two dogs is a handful, but fine," Kerri reasoned. "You'll have the mommy and a little one."

"And break up the family? How about I just pick a favorite, the way my mom took my sister with her when she moved, but not me? And then Dad tells me he's secretly engaged to some woman in London. Like that?" Josh retorted bitterly.

Kerri half lifted her arms, as if she were coming over to

embrace him, but she didn't move. "I didn't know any of that."

"Okay, so, now you know." Josh looked away.

"So what are you going to do? They won't let you keep more than three dogs; that's the rule."

"I don't know," Josh admitted. The question made him tired.

Kerri stood. "Right, then."

"Okay."

He followed her out to her car. Lucy raced out as if she'd never been in the front yard before, her tail wagging, nose down to the frozen ground.

"So," Kerri sighed. Josh sensed a barrier between them, a gap he'd be wise not to bridge, so he halted a few steps from her when she turned. "Merry Christmas, Josh."

"Merry Christmas," he repeated woodenly.

"Don't . . . don't call me, okay? I get you, I understand why you're the way you are, but it's not good for me to be around you." Tears were unexpectedly spilling down her cheeks.

"Kerri."

"No. I mean it. Good-bye, Josh."

Kerri slipped into her car and Josh stood and watched her drive away. Lucy came up to him with a stick in her mouth, dropping it at his feet like a gift, clearly hoping to cheer him up.

Josh went into the house, knowing that for the next several days, maybe even for weeks or months, he'd carry the same empty weight that had settled on his heart after Amanda left, the sense that someone who belonged there was not with him any longer.

The rest of November passed with gray clouds matching Josh's mood. He took Lucy for a few walks, he played with the puppies, he watched Christmas movies. He fell behind in his online coursework. He let dishes pile up in the kitchen, he ignored texts from Wayne. He registered without feeling when the dates crossed into December.

He was sitting at his computer one morning when a conference request popped open on his screen. He accepted it and found himself looking at one of his former teammates on the Blascoe project, a friend who always went by his last name, Quincy. He looked an awful lot like Josh—same short black hair and dark eyes, though Quincy was a lot heavier, having been, in his own words, "In and out of In and Out Burger too many times."

"You hear?" Quincy greeted.

"No, I'm completely out of the loop. What's up?"

"Client *hates* the interface now. There's like six levels of nested menus." Quincy grinned.

"Seriously?" If Blascoe was going to claim that everything was Josh's fault, the damage to his reputation could take a long time to repair.

"You know Blascoe. He keeps adding crap. I swear he lies awake nights thinking of ways to screw everything up. So we had this big crisis meeting and, get this, Suni says, 'We need Josh Michaels.'"

Suni Ohayashi was the number-two person on the project. Josh searched inside himself and yes, it was there—a petty sense of vindication.

"And Blascoe looks at Suni and says, he says"—Quincy dropped his chin and did a passable impression of Blascoe's flat, gruff voice—"'Not an option.'"

Josh nodded. "Huh."

"What did you do to piss off the Blascotoid?"

Josh shrugged. "I wish I knew. Did you see the report I uploaded?"

Quincy shook his head. "No, it wiped when Blascoe delisted you from the project."

"Might have saved everyone some grief."

"I get exactly what you're saying. Maybe, though, with Suni pushing him Blascoe will ask you back."

"Not going to count on that."

"Yeah." Quincy grunted. "You got anything else going on?"

"No. Time of year, not much happening."

"You okay? I mean with not working. How're you doing with all that?" Quincy's expression was pained, as if worried Josh was going to start discussing *feelings* or something.

Josh caught movement out of the corner of his eye. The puppies had decided they needed to roll up the living room rug. They had seized a corner of it and were all tugging in different directions, growling at each other.

"You know, things are great," Josh replied without irony.

A few days later a huge SUV bounced up his driveway,

springs sagging. Josh went to the window and recognized the driver as one of the dads from the ice rink, and when the back door popped open, one of the hockey boys and the little girl ice dancer tumbled out.

"Could we see the puppies?" the little girl asked. She looked as if she'd spent the morning being tuned up at the cuteness factory, with light brown curls, huge brown eyes, and cheeks red from the cold and her excitement. Her brother, a few years older and twice as big, was going to be as huge as the father—both were large, fleshy males, plenty of muscle on the dad, while the boy's bulk was mostly unrealized potential that needed a few years of athletics to shape up.

Josh could not have refused that little girl if she were there asking to burn down his house. He brought the puppies out and when they spotted the children they went from sleep to manic energy in just seconds.

The girl's name was Juliet and the boy was Chuck. The father was Matt. The man's hands were rough and chapped when he and Josh shook, but his smile was a blazing white against his leathery skin, like a cowboy hired to smile in a TV commercial.

The puppies played and tumbled, Cody following Rufus's lead and seizing Chuck's mitten in his little mouth and shaking it with tiny growls. Chuck dropped a rubber ball on the ground and Sophie pounced on it joyously, running off with it. For Sophie, the best thing about new toys was that they were new.

The puppies loved the children—no worries about

socializing these little guys—but it was Lola, though, who seemed most smitten with Juliet, climbing in the little girl's lap and licking her into giggles.

"All Juliet's been talking about is the brown dog with the short ears," Matt said after refusing an offer of coffee. Josh knew what was coming. "Was thinking maybe you'd let me buy her. Time we had a dog and, well, when Juliet sets her mind to something . . ." Matt gave him a rueful grin, those white teeth of his nearly blinding Josh.

"I don't know," Josh said uncomfortably.

Matt sensed something, so he didn't push it. The two men sat in the living room for an hour, watching the children and the puppies play. Chuck rolled around on the floor and let the puppies climb on him like Lilliputians mounting an assault on Gulliver, but for Juliet there was only Lola; the two of them focused completely on each other. When Lola fell asleep in Juliet's arms, it was as an infant, all four limbs pointed slackly up in the air. The expression on Juliet's face was pure bliss.

She handed Lola over without protest, though, when Matt said it was time to go. Josh got the sense that in their family, when the father spoke, the kids did what they were told.

Matt handed Josh a card with a phone number. It said that Matt was a mechanic. "Case you change your mind. Merry Christmas," Matt the mechanic said.

As the SUV drove away, Juliet waved to Josh, smiling. Maybe she was dying of disappointment inside, but her face betrayed nothing but gratitude that she'd had a short time with Lola. Celebrating, and then moving on, Kerri would probably point out if she were standing there. The lesson of the dogs.

When he called the shelter Kerri couldn't come to the phone. Josh left a message. When he called the shelter again and it rolled to voice mail even though it was during operating hours—he pictured Kerri working there by herself, seeing the caller ID, and deciding not to answer.

The window of the shelter was decorated with amateurish but charming paintings of snowmen and holly. Josh peered inside but there was no one at the counter. He opened the door and the same bell jangled.

Kerri's face dropped when she came out of the back room. "Josh," she said. He hated the way his name sounded coming out of her mouth, like it gave her a bad taste.

"Hi, Kerri."

They looked at each other for a moment. She shrugged uncomfortably.

"There's this little girl named Juliet. I want her family to have Lola. You said you guys would handle the adoption."

SIXTEEN

Kerri stared at him for a long moment, her face troubled. *What?* Josh wanted to shout at her. *What else do you want me to do?*

"I'm sorting through some stuff that was donated, would you be willing to help?" Kerri inquired, diffusing the tension a little. Josh nodded mutely and followed her to a back room, where several cardboard boxes gaped open. Kerri told him where to put things: canned food, bagged food, pet toys, "just new toys, not the ones that are chewed and disgusting that people think we'd want." Josh bent down into a box and pulled out what looked like a football uniform for a Chihuahua, complete with shoulder pads and a helmet. "Right, not that, either," Kerri said.

Josh tossed the uniform in the discard pile. He liked that they were doing this simple task and not talking about anything of substance, though as the silence stretched on, he found himself glancing over at Kerri, who was wearing her tight jeans, her brown hair spilling forward as she read the ingredients on a bag of dog food. She eventually decided the food was acceptable.

"So tell me, what changed your mind?" she asked as she put the bag on a shelf.

"A little girl came over."

"And? That's it?"

"Just seeing them together. It's like what you said in your speech about adopting dogs."

"You're telling me I was right," Kerri teased mildly.

"I'm trying *not* to tell you you were right."

"Ahh. Such a guy."

"Plus, well, maybe this seems silly, but it's what Lola wants."

Kerri smiled at him. "And whatever Lola wants," she agreed meaningfully.

"Huh?"

"You don't know it? It's a song." Kerri sang a few verses, waiting for him to get it.

"Um, *My Fair Lady*?"

"*My Fair Lady!*" Kerri laughed. "No, *Damn Yankees*. You so live in a cabin in the mountains."

"Well at least I knew it was a movie."

That made her smile. "The song has been stuck in my head ever since you named her Lola."

"I've been singing 'Grandma Got Run Over by a Reindeer.'"

That one actually got her to laugh. "Anyway . . ." Kerri said. "Look, the puppies are technically your dogs, but there's a process we do here to make sure adopters will make good dog owners. This time of year, a lot of people give dogs as gifts, which we like because it makes room in the shelters, but hate because some people think raising puppies is easy."

Josh nodded. "Yeah, some people can be like that."

"Uh-huh," Kerri dead-panned. "So is it fine with you if these people do an application? I want to make sure all of your puppies wind up in a good home."

"Sure," Josh agreed, not addressing the "all of your puppies" statement. Kneeling, he reached into a box of what looked like six-inch dried snake skins, but were stiff and hard. "What are these?"

"Bison tracheas," Kerri responded simply.

Josh dropped it back into the box. "Yuck."

"The older dogs love 'em. Hey, Josh?"

He looked at her and her blue eyes were serious. "Yeah."

"I didn't think I'd see you again."

"Right. You told me not to call."

"I'm really glad to see you, though. I can't help it."

She was all the way across the room, and Josh just didn't see how he could climb to his feet and get to her, jumping over boxes on the way, without the moment passing. "Me, too," he finally said inadequately.

"I was going to call you, actually," Kerri informed him.

He liked that. "Really?"

She was regarding him carefully. "Yes, because we have a family for Cody."

"Oh."

"There's a family whose dog went blind at six months, and they lost her about a year ago at age fourteen. They know all about how it is to live with a sightless dog, what you need to do. They've had years and years of practice, and they decided they want to adopt a blind dog, to put their skills to good use. Rescue a dog no one else would want, I mean. It's a wonderful opportunity, Josh. Completely unexpected. They saw Cody on the website, they applied, and I interviewed them yesterday. Josh . . . can we give Cody a home? There's a ten-year-old boy, a fenced-in backyard, and a family just waiting to give him love."

They looked at each other, still absurdly all the way across the room from each other. Her smile was warm and sympathetic and he knew he was going to do whatever she wanted. "Yes," he assented, taking in a deep breath and letting it out. "Okay."

A woman named Madelyn showed up to relieve Kerri. Without even realizing he was going to do it, Josh asked if maybe Kerri would like to get something to eat and the two of them drove in separate vehicles to the Evergreen Inn for some Mexican food. They sat in a booth across from each other, the table wide between them. Why did it seem like there was always some barrier in the way?

A Christmas tree adorned a far corner, tight packages in a small pile underneath the blinking lights. Josh wondered if they were empty boxes the owners put out every year. It was a good idea; his own tree always looked forlornly sparse, with just his and Amanda's gifts under it.

Not Amanda, not anymore, he reminded himself.

"We have this thing, a program at the shelter," Kerri told him after they'd ordered. "Basically we suspend adoptions in December until the twenty-third, and then we send every dog to his new forever home with a Christmas collar on. We call it the Dogs of Christmas. It sounds silly, but it really raises some interest in our rescues. We do the Cats of

Christmas, too, but we gave up trying to make them wear Christmas collars."

"I thought you said you hated it when people bought dogs as gifts."

"Yes, I do, personally, but the director likes the program."

"Whatever Lola wants," Josh speculated.

"Exactly."

"Okay, Dogs of Christmas," Josh nodded noncommittally.

"What I was thinking was, we should do that with your dogs. That gives you until the twenty-third, Josh. More than two weeks." Kerri reached out and took his hand. "Will that work for you?"

Josh studied the checkerboard tablecloth. Kerri withdrew her touch when the food arrived, and the cool, lonely feeling in his hand felt portentous—a lot, he knew, was riding on his answer. It wasn't fair, but the choice he was making was pretty clear.

"Fine," he agreed. He reached for the hot sauce, glancing up at her as he did so. She was smiling, and it made his heart soar.

When they walked to the parking lot after dinner, it was starting to snow. The flakes danced in the multicolored lights in the shop windows, swirling in the light breeze and starting to build on the rooftops. From somewhere unseen speakers quietly played "Frosty the Snowman." For a moment Josh was transported back in time and was a child, thrilled at the decorations, walking this same sidewalk, hearing the same music from probably the same hidden speakers. And then he was back, strolling next to this woman, equally as captivated now as he had been then.

"A white Christmas!" Kerri exclaimed, holding her tongue out to catch a snowflake.

"Maybe. Or maybe tomorrow it's eighty degrees," Josh speculated.

"Always looking on the bright side," Kerri responded playfully. She pushed against him and, in the process, slipped her arm through his.

They stopped at her car. "Could I maybe come out for Cody Wednesday? I'll call the family tomorrow."

"You said the twenty-third," Josh objected.

"Right, I did say that, but for Cody I don't think it makes any sense to wait, do you? The sooner he gets used to his new home, the better."

"I guess. Sure. Yes." Josh had made his decision, but hadn't been prepared for the reality of Wednesday. The day before Christmas Eve still felt far enough away to him as to be nearly forever, though it was only fifteen days.

"You're doing the right thing, Josh, and it's the hard thing and I'm proud of you." Kerri reached up and touched his face, and he kissed her, and this, too, was a complete surprise. The way she clutched him in the parking lot, the snow in her hair turning to water under his hand, warmed him through his whole body. When their lips broke apart, they were both smiling, though her teeth were chattering a little.

"You're cold," he declared.

"Freezing," she admitted.

"Okay, go, get warm."

"Right." She kissed him again, a quick one, then jumped into her car. "I'll talk to you tomorrow," she said.

"Tomorrow? What's tomorrow?"

"When you call me," she said brightly. She shut her car door and drove off.

Josh was vibrating with a new, unnamed energy that made him want to do something impulsive, like go into a bar and shout that he was buying a round of drinks for the house. "Merry Christmas!" he boisterously greeted people walking in downtown Evergreen. He passed a flower shop and wondered if now would be a good time for roses, then decided to hit a gift shop instead, feeling as generous as Scrooge buying a goose for the Cratchit family. Would Kerri like a basket filled with teas and cookies? A music box shaped like an old phonograph player? A mouse that played a few stanzas of "O Christmas Tree" when you squeezed his nose?

He decided maybe just a card. The one he picked had a poem on the front that he'd first read in high school. Josh remembered that all the girls liked it because they said it was about someone looking for love and finally finding it.

The Penny
I tossed a penny into the well
And for quite some the copper fell

Without a sound returned to ear
And just when I'd begun to fear
Such small impact I'd never hear
A tiny call from down below
Announced arrival of my throw.

Looking for love? As far as Josh could tell the poem was about somebody dropping a penny into a well. Kerri was a woman, though, and they saw the hidden meaning in stuff like this. He bought the card and took it home and put Kerri's name on the envelope. It was the kind of card with all the words on the front—inside the card, fresh, cream-colored paper waited blankly for him to write something profound.

Two hours later and the inside of the card was still blank.

The next morning the snow was a four-inch layer on the ground, some of the driest, fluffiest powder Josh had ever seen. He opened the back door for the puppies and they stopped as dead as if they'd just spotted Waldo the cat, the white blanket an intimidating mystery.

For Lucy, though, it was a joyous transformation. She leaped over the puppies like a steeplechase horse, landing in an explosion of white and going down on one shoulder to drive herself like a snowplow across the yard. Her puppies, following the *when in doubt stick with Mom* dictum, took a few tentative steps. They were shocked and intimidated as their paws sank into the snow, but the magnetic properties of Lucy's maternal pull overcame their apprehension. Testing it like people checking the temperature of bath water, they cautiously went out into the white stuff, sniffing suspiciously. Lucy was spinning and leaping: *Come on, this is what dogs do in these situations!* They scampered after her, more and more emboldened, each discovering the delights of snow on his and her own, rolling and tumbling in ecstasy. Cody romped, too, Rufus close, not to guide him, but just to be nearby while Cody went as crazy as everyone else.

Josh brushed the snow off his steps with a broom and sat with a cup of coffee, more happy than he'd been in a long time. From time to time one of the dogs would break away and run over to him as if to say, *Isn't this the best stuff ever?* Lucy climbed into the dog pile to be with them and they all went after her. Her teats were dry and withdrawn, now, so it was just play they were interested in, biting at their mommy as if Lucy were a chew toy. She expertly flipped them on their backs in the snow, and then they'd be on their feet, coming right back at their mommy dog, their little tails wagging.

As if a signal had been passed between them, they all calmed down at about the same time, panting and sprawling in the snow, chewing at it, raising their heads drowsily when Josh came for them. As he moved Lola and Sophie into the house, their brothers roused themselves and followed of their own volition, clambering awkwardly up the stairs and bounding in pursuit of Josh down the hall, feet leaving tiny puddles of melt water that glittered on the floor like jewels.

They settled without protest into their box. Lucy took up her favorite position in the living room.

"They went berserk," Josh told Kerri on the phone. "You should have seen it."

As he said it, he caught himself wondering, yeah, *why weren't you here to see it?*

How could he entice Kerri to be here more often, to stay with him longer when she did come? A review of their relationship thus far consisted mostly of the two of them saying good-bye to each other.

Kerri said she'd be out the next morning. "I'll see you then!" she said gaily before they hung up.

Why aren't I seeing you tonight? Josh wondered. Why didn't he think to ask her to dinner?

Because, he knew, he'd put a lot of thought into inviting her over for dinner the last time and she'd immediately bolted across the state line. Wyoming. What kind of signal did it send that her excuse was Wyoming?

He pulled out the card he'd bought. Still blank. Why hadn't he bought one that had words on the inside, too? *Dear Kerri*, he could write. *Please don't go to Wyoming again.* Or, better: *Don't go to Wyoming without me.*

He put the card away, knowing nothing would occur to him. Maybe he'd use it on Mother's Day or something.

A low fog hung in the trees the next morning, as if clouds, caught sleeping on the ground, had gotten trapped in the branches as they tried to rise back up to the sky. Josh had been awake for hours and had showered and shaved and was wearing a pair of jeans to be casual but they were clean and new and looked, he hoped, nice. His long-sleeved shirt had a software company logo because he wanted her to remember he had a good job. Well, usually, anyway. Kerri's car pulled into his driveway and Lucy gave a lazy "wuff," just one, as if to say, *I could scare her off if I wanted to.*

Josh made himself wait until she knocked on the door. The puppies had taken over the living room and were wrestling each other over one of the throw pillows.

"Okay, Cody, this is it," Josh proclaimed. Cody didn't show any signs of hearing or caring about his name.

"Hi! It's good to see you! You here for Cody?" Josh asked.

"Yes," Kerri replied.

He was going to kiss her, had planned to all morning, but something in her manner, something diffident, gave him pause.

"Your friend called. The one with the little girl. For Lola. We took their application yesterday," Kerri said. She wasn't looking at Josh. "Hey, puppies," Kerri greeted softly, sliding to her knees on the living-room floor. The puppies forgot about the pillow wars and piled into her.

"What's wrong?" Josh asked.

Kerri looked at him. Her eyes were fearful, almost—hurt and fearful. She slowly stood, bringing a folded piece of paper out of her pocket.

"This was on our bulletin board, but there was stuff stuck over it and I didn't see it until Madelyn came in this morning and organized it. Oh, Josh," Kerri said.

She handed him the piece of paper. There was a picture of Lucy on it, along with a few words in large font:

Dog Lost/Stolen

"Lucy"

Pregnant or nursing puppies.

Call Serena.

I love my dog.

Reward.

SEVENTEEN

Josh held the homemade poster as he sank wearily down in a chair, his legs suddenly weak. Lucy, sensing something, came over to him, her nails clicking on the floor, and laid her head in his lap, looking up into his eyes. He absently stroked between her ears, staring at the poster as if it contained words he couldn't comprehend.

"I'm so sorry, Josh," Kerri whispered. She stood in front of him, looking down, her eyes moist. "I know this is . . . a shock. How hard this is."

Lost. *Stolen.* Josh tried to picture the sort of people who would treat Lucy as some sort of weapon in the war between them. Serena had "dumped" Lucy, Ryan had claimed. Now Lucy was "stolen."

Who knew what had really happened? Who knew the truth, besides Lucy?

"It says September," Josh noted dully.

"Sorry?"

"See? Your fax machine put a date on it. September twenty-second. This is December thirteenth. *December.*"

"I'm not sure I understand," Kerri replied slowly.

"That's almost three months."

"Right, but Josh, does that matter? Lucy has a person she belongs to."

"And so nothing that has happened here counts for anything," Josh responded bitterly. He stood up, Lucy tracking him with anxious eyes. To have something to do he flung another piece of wood on the fire, which snapped and spat sparks back at him.

"Everything *counts,* Josh. You took in a dog and newborn puppies and did a wonderful job."

"Sure."

Kerri bit her lip. "You're not . . . you're not saying you won't give Lucy back?"

Josh looked away.

"Josh?"

"You said I would always have Lucy."

"Yes but I didn't *know.*"

For some reason he remembered Amanda carrying her boxes out to her car on the last day. He wouldn't help, just watched moodily as she struggled. The feeling was the same: arbitrarily and without fair warning, a part of him was being ripped out.

Except this time he could do something about it.

Kerri watched his face harden and put a hand to her mouth.

"Josh. *No.*"

He still wasn't looking in her direction. There was a long moment, and then he glanced at her because of a strange sound. She was crying.

"Josh, you have to call her. You have to. Because if you don't . . ."

"You'll what? You'll do what?" he demanded, more harshly than he'd intended.

She shook her head wildly. "I don't know what. I just know, if you don't, it means you're not the man I think you are."

"So it's another test?"

"A test?"

"You always ask me to choose between you and my dogs," he said bitterly.

"Oh God. Josh . . ."

They stood there, and Josh went from feeling fierce to deflated. He reached down and picked up Cody—he was drained and empty enough to do this now. He held Cody nose-to-nose with Rufus, who looked up drowsily from his nap, seeming to focus with only the eye in the center of his brown spot, the other one half-lidded. "Say good-bye to Cody, Rufus."

Rufus, missing the significance, put his head back down. Cody struggled a little in his hands.

"You're going to have a good home. A happy home, Cody. They know how to take care of blind doggies there. You be a good little dog now."

Josh went out the front door and Kerri followed him. The gloomy day matched his mood perfectly. He watched without comment as Kerri opened her hatchback, noting that the sagging, duct-taped dog carrier now appeared to be collapsing on the right side instead of the left. Kerri took Cody from his arms and placed the warm little bundle in the carrier and shut the door. Cody sniffed the new situation curiously.

"Right," Kerri said. "Bye."

"Bye."

Neither their bodies nor their glances touched each other, and Josh didn't watch as the Subaru turned and drove down his driveway.

That was the ultimate weapon women wielded, wasn't it? In the end, they could always just leave.

The puppies woke up that afternoon, but only Rufus seemed to notice they were missing Cody. He sniffed around the house, starting with the living room, then moved down the hallway and into the bedrooms, searching for a lost little dog.

"He's gone, Rufus. Cody's gone," Josh explained, his throat tight as he said the words. Rufus, of course, didn't understand. He picked up the little dog and rocked him in his arms, gazing mournfully down at him. Rufus stared back with what Josh felt was hurt accusation in his eyes.

Why did it seem as if this was Josh's pattern, repeated over and over? A breakup, a splintering of a previously inviolate relationship, with Josh left in the middle by himself to deal with the fragments.

That night he pulled the puppies into bed with him, Lucy watching with stern disapproval. He had in mind a mournful cuddle but the little dogs were so thrilled to be able to play in the covers that Josh found himself laughing despite everything. Another thing dogs could do for people—lift the mood with their mad antics no matter what the situation.

A conference request the next morning gave him a start. It was Suni Ohayashi, the number-two person on the Blascoe project. Suni was known for being competent, if a bit cold and businesslike.

"Merry Christmas, Josh," Suni greeted.

"Merry Christmas, Suni," Josh echoed automatically.

"I don't know if you've heard, but I've been appointed project manager," Suni advised.

"No, I didn't know that. So Blascoe?"

Suni nodded. "I'm replacing Gordon Blascoe."

"Ah."

"Are you available to come back on when we gear up after New Year's?"

Josh smiled. "I could be," he admitted.

"Your report was exactly right. We need your simplicity, the way you always figure out the right thing to do."

"Thank you."

"Good, then. See you after the first. Merry Christmas again."

"Same to you, Suni."

When they signed off he had the impulse to share the news with Kerri, but in the end didn't try to call.

Josh marked the holiday traditions as grimly as if they were high school homework assignments. He trudged out to joylessly buy gifts for Janice's boys and for his mom—everyone else got cards. He stood and drank cider and impassively watched carolers sing in front of the hardware store. He ordered a gift for Kerri—he'd give it to her whether she wanted to see him or not.

Whenever he thought about Kerri, a resentful stubbornness rose up inside him. He'd given up Cody and agreed to surrender the rest of his puppies, but that wasn't enough. She wanted Lucy, too.

"My dog, Lucy. You are my dog," Josh told her. She looked back with what Josh took to be an *of course* expression.

Knowing he was going to lose them, Josh engaged in determined play with the puppies. He'd drag them across the floor with a towel, each of them growling. He'd roll with them on his bed, or toss a ball. Only the girls, Sophie and Lola, chased the thing—the boys seemed to feel if he'd thrown it away it must not be a toy worth playing with.

Always, Rufus seemed subdued in these activities. He'd be tugging on the towel and then abruptly stop, wandering over to the front door to sniff under the crack, or heading back to the box to probe its corners with his muzzle. He took more naps then the other dogs, and Lucy, as if responding to some subconscious signal, started sniffing and licking Rufus, even though she'd pretty much stopped grooming the puppies when she weaned them.

"Are you okay, Rufus? Are you sick or something?" Josh asked, holding the little guy up and peering at him. But Josh knew there was no virus. "You miss him, don't you?" Josh whispered. "Me, too, Rufus. Me, too." Without Cody, Rufus had lost his purpose. Same for Josh when Amanda left. "Same thing," he told Rufus. "Exactly the same thing."

A week before Christmas Eve, during a white-out blizzard that made whistles out of his doorjambs and sucked air up the chimney until his coals glowed like the bowl of a pipe, his sister Janice phoned.

"I was just thinking about our last conversation," she informed him. "About how we need to get together more often."

"Yeah?" The day before the UPS man had brought out Kerri's Christmas present—a huge cardboard box, nearly the size of an oven—and the dogs were attacking it as if there were beefsteaks inside, gnawing industriously on the corners. He had probably a hundred dollars' worth of chew toys strewn about the living room, but since the arrival of the box the puppies were interested in nothing else.

"Why don't you come up for Christmas? Or New Year's? The boys have two weeks off with no school and no hockey, thank God. We could go skiing and sledding."

"Sounds like fun, but I have this dog issue," Josh demurred.

"The puppies? Aren't they old enough to be adopted, yet?"

"Yes, that's happening on the twenty-third. But the mother dog, Lucy. I think it would really confuse her to leave her here by herself or in a kennel right after giving away her pups."

"Oh. You're keeping the mother?"

"Looks that way, yeah." Josh's eyes strayed to the lost-dog poster, still sitting on the side table where he'd left it.

They talked about a few more things. "I got a really nice card from Amanda," Janice finally offered casually.

"Oh?" He wondered if this was why his sister was really calling.

"Do you talk to her?"

"What did the card say?"

"Oh, you know, Merry Christmas, but she also talked about how great Christmas morning always was at your house, how you made coffee and heated up the rolls. It was just, I don't know. A little melancholy."

Josh looked over at Rufus, who, as usual, had been the first to stop in attacking the box and was lying by himself on the floor, his eyes closed.

"Huh," Josh grunted.

"She said you told her that she rescued Christmas for you. What did Amanda mean by that?"

"Oh, you know," Josh replied uncomfortably.

"I really don't," Janice pressed, something in her voice suggesting she knew she wasn't going to like the answer.

"Well, it was right before Christmas when you and Mom left." Josh swallowed back the rise of painful emotions. "And so it was just Dad and me that morning. All your gifts were out, but you didn't come. It was pretty brutal."

"God, I know. Dad wouldn't let us come home. We spent that Christmas in a hotel."

"What do you mean?" Josh asked sharply. "'Wouldn't let you.' You guys *left*."

"Well, yeah," Janice agreed haltingly. "We left because of that huge fight. You were skiing, I think, so you didn't see, but when they started hitting each other I got in the middle. It was really bad, Josh. But you know all this."

"No, I don't. They *hit* each other?" Josh replied incredulously.

"Yeah, we had to get out of there."

"I just remember getting dropped off by my friends from the ski trip and you were leaving."

"Well, but you didn't want to come," Janice reasoned.

"I didn't want you to *go*," Josh replied through clenched teeth. "There's a difference."

"It was awful," Janice murmured, remembering.

"Dad was in this silent rage after that," Josh told her after a moment. "He wouldn't talk to me. Except Christmas morning, after we'd opened presents, and then he tells me about Pamela, that they're going to get married as soon as the divorce is settled."

"I'm so sorry, Josh. I guess I never thought about what it was like for you. I was kind of focused on myself."

"Christmas was ruined for me, then. Because of what happened. Until Amanda."

"We had good Christmases after that one," Janice objected.

"Not for me," Josh retorted. "Never with the whole family. Never in a place I could call *home*."

"Josh, you were seventeen. I mean, that seems old enough—"

"Old enough to have the family ripped apart?" Josh challenged.

After a pause, Janice sighed. "It wasn't . . . God, I know you felt like it was your job to keep us all together. But sometimes you just need to let things go."

His eyes were drawn to Lucy. "Right," he said bitterly.

"I'm really, really sorry. I know how much it affected you. I mean, I didn't get it at the time, probably no one did, but

I've seen how you struggle with it. I'm just . . . sorry. For everything."

"Merry Christmas, Janice."

She drew in a breath at this rebuff. "Okay, Merry Christmas. I love you, Josh."

"No, no, wait," Josh said. "I . . . I love you, too, Janice. I'm sorry, too." He gripped the phone, not trusting himself to speak.

Janice waited for him to say more, and when he didn't, breezily suggested he plan to get up to Portland sometime soon. He managed to say he would.

The next day, the wind gone but the snow still coming down, his new friend Matt the mechanic called to thank him for letting his family adopt Lola. "Juliet is especially excited. She can't sleep and it's not even Christmas Eve."

"It wasn't my choice, actually," Josh informed him. "The shelter gets to decide."

"They said you wanted us. I'm real grateful. You ever need a favor, you just ask."

"Good because, I'd . . . I'd like to visit. To see Lola from time to time, I mean. If that would be okay," Josh replied, not knowing he was going to ask until he did so.

"Of course!" Matt replied.

Josh hung up wondering why the conversation hadn't made him feel any better.

Another call was from the animal shelter. Josh snatched it up when he saw the caller ID, but it was the woman named Madelyn. "Just calling to let you know we have approved homes for all of your puppies," Madelyn chimed happily.

Josh didn't really know the woman but he felt a bilious resentment rise up within him. "All the rest of them," he corrected testily.

"Sorry?"

"Is Kerri there?"

Madelyn's silent pause was as full of heavy meaning as a growl. "She asked me to make the call," Madelyn finally informed him primly.

"Fine. Tell her Rufus is acting depressed, okay?"

"Rufus is depressed," Madelyn repeated before ringing off, making it sound as if she thought Josh was an idiot.

Wayne called because it was snowing and he wanted to make sure Josh hadn't "gone all Donner party."

"Why don't you and Leigh come over for dinner to find out?" Josh said in a cartoon-evil voice, but his heart wasn't in the banter. Wayne said he was headed to Leigh's crazy parents' house for two weeks, "so watch the TV to see if I kill somebody."

"Have fun."

"You want to come with us?"

"Yes. Yes I do," Josh replied.

Wayne laughed maniacally. "Merry Christmas, Dude," he said.

He checked caller ID a few times a day to see if Kerri had called, even when he'd been home all day and would have heard the phone. On December 19th, Christmas less than a week away, he went into town for supplies. While he was in the store the snow stopped and the sun came out, so that the roads were slick and black next to the snowdrifts, like warm chocolate syrup drizzled on vanilla ice cream. Car tires made ripping sounds on the wet pavement, sounding to Josh like Velcro being pulled apart.

When he got home his caller ID said he'd missed two calls, but they weren't from Kerri. They were from Amanda.

There were no messages.

He didn't know why she was calling, but the fact that she had didn't lift his mood—if anything, he felt vague adumbrations of troubles ahead. She could still hurt him, he knew. What was she up to?

December twentieth was clear and warm, the snow melting from the tree limbs in a solid rain or falling in huge, muffled clumps.

You always figure out the right thing to do, Suni had told him. Really? Was that really who Josh Michaels was? *I know you felt like it was your job to keep us all together,* his sister said.

Whose job was it, then? Who was going to do it if Josh didn't?

Josh knew he had a phone call to make, and this was the reason for the black scowl he wore. He pictured himself doing it, thinking about how it would turn out, but he really didn't know how to forecast on such an unpredictable topic. When a man phoned a woman, no matter what the reason, he quickly lost control of the direction of the conversation. That had always been his experience, anyway.

Okay, the hell with it. Time to call.

Josh dialed, steeling himself for when she answered.

"Hello," he greeted cautiously. "Is this Serena?"

EIGHTEEN

Who is calling, please?" Serena replied, pleasant but cautious.

"Um, I'm calling about the lost dog."

Josh closed his eyes at her gasp.

"Oh my God. Did you find her? Did you find Lucy?" Serena asked urgently, her voice cracking.

"I don't know. I mean, your poster has been up since when, September?"

"She's . . . she has a black nose, and she's brown, and her back is black fur," Serena babbled. "And she was pregnant. Does your dog look like she's nursing puppies?"

Not anymore, Josh thought to himself. "Why don't you just tell me what happened," he replied steadily.

"Sorry?"

"Your poster says 'lost slash stolen.' What does that mean?"

"What difference does it make?" Serena demanded.

"I'm just trying to understand, okay?"

She took a deep, careful breath. "Okay, sorry. Okay. I travel for my work. Not a lot, but some. I was out of town but my neighbor was taking care of Lucy. And then she went to feed her and the back gate was open and Lucy was just gone." Serena was weeping again, nearly silently. "I took the next plane home. I was supposed to get her microchipped, I know that, but I was just so busy."

"Why do you say lost *or* stolen?"

"Um, I can't prove anything, but I used to live with this guy, Ryan. We broke up and it wasn't, I mean, he didn't take it very well. Like, threatening. And right around the time Lucy disappeared, someone saw him in the neighborhood. *Thought* they saw him. Like he was hanging around my place. And then Ryan's like, gone. I knocked and left a note for him, three times right after Luce vanished. I went again not long ago and now there's a lock on his front door, a padlock, and a notice from his landlord, and his cell has been disconnected this whole time."

Josh briefly closed his eyes, picturing Serena driving up to the cabin Ryan had been renting right next door. The properties in this area were pretty big—Josh owned sixty acres of land—but still, at some point, Serena was probably no more than a hundred yards away. How different would his life be if she'd shown up when the puppies were still nursing? Would he even still have them?

"You didn't leave your dog with Ryan?" Josh probed.

"God, no. Why do you ask that?" Serena responded suspiciously.

"It's nothing. Just trying to get a sense of events as they transpired in this particular situation," he answered, stalling the inevitable with verbiage.

"When did you find your dog? Do you think it could be Lucy?"

"My name is Josh Michaels, does that mean anything to you?"

"No. Josh Michaels. No, sorry. Why, should it?"

"No. God." Josh sat down on a kitchen stool, putting his hand to his face. Across the room Lucy was watching him, her dark eyes seeming, to Josh, to radiate concern. "I'm pretty sure this is your dog."

"Oh my God. Really? You have no idea what this means to me!"

"The thing is, Ryan gave her to me."

"What? You're a friend of Ryan?" she cried.

"No, I'm . . ."

"You listen to me," Serena grated, her voice choking. "He stole my dog which means *you* stole my dog, and I'll call the police, you'll be *arrested*—"

"No, it wasn't like that," Josh snapped, his voice sharp. He listened to Serena pant at the other end of the line. "Okay? Just listen to me. He told me you gave him the dog, like to watch."

"I did not *give him my dog*," she spat.

"I know. I know that now, anyway. So here's what happened." Josh walked her through the night Ryan had shown up with Lucy. When he got to the part about her obvious pregnancy, Serena interrupted. "She had the puppies? Are they okay?"

Haltingly, Josh explained about the stillborn delivery, and the small miracle of the puppies in the box in the back of his truck. "So a few days ago this friend from the shelter brought me your poster," Josh finished.

"Thank you. Thank you for rescuing Lucy and for taking care of her," Serena sobbed. "This is the most wonderful phone call of my life. Bless you, bless you."

"Sure," Josh responded faintly.

"I have a sister in Parker. She could come up and get Lucy. I'm not in town until the day before Christmas Eve, I could . . . I really can't get back before then."

"Look, I don't mind taking care of her until then."

"I want my dog back!"

"Yes, okay, but I'm just saying, why not wait until you're back in town?" Josh explained about the Dogs of Christmas, how all the puppies would be leaving the twenty-third, the same day Serena would be back. "I just think it would be easier if Lucy doesn't leave until the puppies are gone. I mean, I'm picturing them watching their mom drive off and I'm thinking, why put them through that? What do you think, would that be okay?"

And in his mind, Josh was standing by the big ponderosa pine tree, watching his own mother drive away, Janice waving from the passenger window. Josh did not wave back.

"You've got such a warm heart," Serena praised, her voice nearly giddy. "Yes, of course. For her puppies? That's wonderful."

Josh gave her his address. She connected the dots. "God, I was so close. I thought about knocking on some neighbors' doors. If only I had."

"Well, but the puppies weren't ready to be weaned then," Josh objected.

There was a pause while they both decided the matter wasn't worth fighting over now.

After the phone call, Josh went over to where Lucy lay on her pillow and buried his face in her fur. She sighed, laying her head back down.

The next morning, Madelyn from the shelter called. "Hi, Josh," she sang merrily, as if they were old friends.

He batted aside her cheerful salutations with grunts, waiting for her to state her business. "So, I was hoping to swing up to your place today," she finally advised.

"What for?"

"Thought it'd be a good time. We're really busy tomorrow getting ready for the adoption event on Friday."

"What do you mean?"

"I said, I thought I should pick the puppies up today because we're going to be jammed up tomorrow. The Dogs of Christmas."

"Come out here and pick up the puppies." He felt dismissed, discounted, this woman he didn't even know breezily informing him she wanted to come take away his dog family a day early out of *convenience*.

"Yes, would this afternoon be okay?"

"No."

She heard a stone wall backing up that single word, and responded cautiously. "Oh. Right. Uh, so when could I come out to pick them up?"

"You can't," Josh said shortly.

"I see," Madelyn replied, plainly not seeing.

"Thanks for calling," Josh told her. He hung up with cold

satisfaction, not even bothering to walk away. It took only a few minutes before the phone rang again. He picked it up.

"What's going on?" Kerri demanded.

"It's good to hear your voice, too," Josh greeted.

"Cut it out. We've got families who have been promised those puppies, Josh. You *can't* back out now."

"Did I say that?"

"Sorry?"

"I didn't say I was backing out. But why can't they come out here? Why does it have to happen in a shelter? Don't you think the dogs would be happier if they were in their own home while this was going on? I think it would be easier for them to see their brothers and sisters drive off if they're home. Lucy can comfort them if they're upset."

"I don't think that matters."

"Well, I do."

Kerri sighed, surrendering. "I guess Madelyn could bring out the paperwork."

"No, I guess she couldn't."

"Josh."

"I'm doing it, Kerri, but I'm doing it my way and the dogs don't know Madelyn, they know you. Okay? You do the paperwork. Come on out for the big Christmas sale, we're open all day Friday."

"We'll have to call everybody, make sure they can get there," Kerri objected.

"Sounds like a plan," Josh stated agreeably.

Kerri was silent a moment. "Fine. I'll see you Friday morning," she said coldly.

The warm weather quickly stripped Denver of its snow layer, though at Josh's elevation the white stuff sublimated much more slowly and never left the shadowed areas, where it went from fluffy powder to gritty, granular piles of ice. Josh let the puppies play in it and threw heavy snowballs at the trees, which Lucy found exciting but was an action over the puppies' heads, both figuratively and literally. The chatter on the news was whether the weak storm front that was slated to arrive on Friday night would have enough moisture to make it a white Christmas.

Josh spent the last day with the dogs as if he were one of them. He rolled with them on the floor, he played with their toys, he sprawled out on the rug to lie with them when they napped. Lucy kept sniffing him as if trying to pick up the scent of whatever mental disorder had Josh behaving so oddly, but for Josh it was a perfect time, a day to capture in his mind and remember forever.

When he put the dogs to bed in their box that night, he sang them to sleep with "Silent Night," and he would have sworn that as they closed their eyes, they all gave him a drowsy look of thanks.

"Good night, puppies. Tonight's the last night. You okay, Rufus?" Josh petted the little dog with the spot over his eye, who was curled up against little Lola but not really sleeping. "I know you miss Cody," Josh told him, "but you'll be with a new family tomorrow and you're supposed to cherish the time we had together and not mourn its passing." The words sounded hollow and, well, stupid to Josh. This had been a perfect day with his dogs and tomorrow would not be. *That* was the lesson here.

He woke up early the next morning, showered and shaved, and then cleaned the house.

He didn't spend all morning standing in the window, but Kerri would not know that because that's what he was doing when she pulled in the driveway. She got out of her car, a clipboard in her hand, and stared at him standing there without waving to him.

"Here we go." Josh sighed.

NINETEEN

I have the people scheduled at staggered times," Kerri advised when he opened the door. "But they don't always come when they are supposed to, which means several could show up at once. If that happens, could you maybe help with the paperwork? It's just signing the forms—everyone has already been through the approval process."

"Good to see you, too, Kerri," Josh muttered under his breath. It *was* good to see her; she had on the white sweater from Thanksgiving and black pants and looked striking.

"Sorry?"

"Nothing." He walked over to her and she held her clipboard across her chest like a shield. The message was clear, and Josh kept several feet between them, though a chance flicker of breeze granted him the favor of a fleeting waft of her perfume.

Sure lost interest in me in a hurry, he thought to himself.

"First one is Sophie," Kerri said, her tone perfunctory and all business. She reached into her purse and pulled out a green collar with a little red ball on it. "This is the Christmas collar, isn't it cute?"

"Do I let the people in my house, or bring the puppies out here, or what?"

"Maybe when they come, just go in and get their dog," Kerri suggested. "You can put the collar on them right before you bring them out. Experience tells us that the puppies will chew them right off each other if we put them on too soon."

"Okay." Josh shoved his hands in his pockets. "Think it will be a white Christmas?"

She gave him a level gaze and he looked away from it, hating the sick way his stomach dropped in the face of the coldness in her eyes.

Mercifully, a car pulled up just then. A middle-aged couple in the front seat peered at the house with the uncertain expressions of people who weren't sure they were in the right place.

"Are you the Sherwoods?" Kerri asked.

"Yeah, is this the place for the dogs?" the man replied.

"I'm Jody and he's Andy," the woman elaborated with a glance at her husband. They all shook hands, Josh looking them up and down. They were attractive people, but how did he know they would be good parents to Sophie?

"Our youngest just left for college," Andy explained as if answering Josh's mentally expressed question. "So we've got sort of an empty nest."

"You think she'd rather have a toy mouse or a ball?" Jody asked, peering into a bag.

"Probably either." Josh smiled, remembering how many

dog toys he'd brought home for Lucy after his first trip to the store.

"It's Sophie," Kerri informed Josh, her bossy tone of voice a perfect match to the officious-looking clipboard in her hands.

"I'll get her," Josh said, his voice matching Kerri's.

Inside, the dogs had decided the time had come for a determined assault on the bookshelf and had dragged a T. Jefferson Parker novel out to destroy. "Hey, you guys," Josh chided gently. He found a Thomas Perry and a Michael Connelly in fairly chewed condition, too. They had good taste in crime fiction. "Okay, Sophie," he whispered gently. He picked up the squirming little dog. "Say good-bye to your brothers and sister." He snapped the collar in place and Sophie began twisting her head, trying to get at this new toy.

The puppies were busy wrestling over a torn book jacket and took no interest in their sister's departure. Their mother was lying on her pillow and Josh held Sophie out to Lucy for a nose-to-nose farewell. Sophie licked and nipped at her mother, who looked away in disgust. She got to her feet, though, when Josh opened the front door, bounding out to greet Kerri and to sniff at the Sherwood family.

"We're all set here," Kerri called, waving the clipboard at Josh.

"There you are, there's our baby," Jody crooned. She pulled Sophie out of Josh's hands and the puppy kissed her face. "I love the white tip at the end of her tail, her little white tip." She laughed. "Look at the collar, isn't it the cutest?"

"Very cute," Andy affirmed drolly.

Josh swallowed and nodded, not trusting himself to speak. Jody gave Sophie a toy kangaroo. It seemed pretty silly to have a kangaroo in Colorado, but Sophie didn't seem to mind.

As the car pulled away, little Sophie sat in Jody's lap, staring at Josh and Lucy in what he felt certain was complete befuddlement, and that's what broke him. He turned away from Kerri so she wouldn't see his tears. Lucy came to his side, nosing his hand in concern.

"Josh . . ." Kerri said softly.

"Why do we do this?" he grated hoarsely. "Did you see Sophie's face? Why do we think we have the right to break up families?"

"We're not breaking families, we're making families," Kerri said.

Josh forced himself under control, taking his breaths in deep gulps.

Kerri was watching him steadily with her clear blue eyes. "I know that right now it seems sad that the puppies are leaving each other, but I promise you that Sophie's going to be so, so happy. They all are."

"How can you know that?"

"Because being with us is a dog's purpose, Josh. We bred the species to be that way—the ones that didn't want to live with people weren't allowed to reproduce. So after thousands of years, it's literally in their blood. If you could see some of the feral dogs we pick up, you'd understand. Living away from humans, even in a dog pack, is unnatural for them. They aren't happy."

"Is this another one of your speeches you give?"

She blinked as if he'd tried to slap her. "No," she replied in a small voice.

A familiar SUV pulled in the driveway. It was Matt, Josh's neighbor, with his little girl, Juliet. Kerri handed him another Christmas collar. "I'll get Lola," Josh told them. Lucy wagged at the new arrivals, sitting and letting Juliet pet her.

When he came back out of the house, something told him to put Lola down on the lawn, and when he did Juliet knelt and the puppy bounded across the yellow grass and straight into the little girl's arms. Part of Josh's resentment melted away as he watched their joyous coming together. Whatever else happened that day, this part felt right.

"That was like watching a dog food commercial," Josh remarked, joining the adult people. Matt was signing Kerri's paper.

"It's all she asked for this Christmas," Matt replied. He handed the clipboard to Kerri and held his hand out to Josh. "Much obliged."

"Sure," Josh said.

As they left, Josh crossed his arms. It felt colder.

"I have a feeling that Lola's going to be hugged for forty-eight straight hours," Kerri observed happily.

Josh didn't reply.

"Did that help? Seeing the little girl, how happy the two of them were together?"

Josh couldn't think of an answer to her question that wouldn't carry a sharp edge to it. He resented being talked down to. He wasn't a mental case.

"We get dogs all year round," Kerri told him. "You can have one or two or three, anytime."

"I don't want future dogs, I want my dogs," Josh responded dully. *Nobody understood.*

"Next one is Rufus," Kerri said after a long silence, the hostility firmly reestablished between them.

As it turned out, Rufus was not next. Instead, after a long wait, Oliver's new owner came, an older man whose craggy face broke into a wide smile when Josh brought the little dog out. He looked like a lot of the men of Evergreen, wearing layered mountain garb and heavy boots. His SUV had a multifunction rack on top with clamps for skis and for a kayak, and there was a large, heavy-looking backpack visible through the rear window.

"You a hiker?" Josh guessed.

"Yep," the man replied, his focus on his new puppy. "This little guy and I are going to hit the trails as soon as he's old enough."

Josh glanced probingly at Kerri. She gave a tiny shrug. "Bye, Oliver," Josh murmured as he handed him over, the small Christmas bulb jiggling Oliver's collar.

"He's retired and his wife just died of cancer," Kerri volunteered as the man drove off.

Josh looked at her.

"Oliver's new daddy," she explained. "He'll love him and they'll be the centers of each other's worlds."

"You're pretty good at this. Finding the right people, I mean. A shop-a-holic for Sophie and an explorer for Oliver."

"Right, lots of practice, I guess."

He nodded and glanced at the front window of the house and there was little Rufus, the last puppy, watching them. Josh pressed his lips together. The poor little guy, all alone.

"Josh," Kerri whispered. She half-started toward him, then stopped herself, remembering that she had written him off. "I'm so sorry."

"Yeah." Josh reached down and stroked Lucy's head. She was gazing into his eyes with what he thought looked like sympathy. The mommy dog seemed oddly untroubled by the day's departures. Wasn't she grieving the loss of her children? Was Josh the only one who cared?

"I can't get a signal," Kerri complained, frowning at her cell phone.

"That's what happens up here. There's a place in the back where you can sometimes get reception if you want. I can show you."

"Could I just use your landline instead? I want to see if I can reach the people who are coming for Rufus."

"Sure. Come on, Lucy."

When they opened the front door Rufus was right there, jumping up and licking his mommy's mouth. Lucy put up with about ten seconds of it and then turned away.

"Hey, Rufus," Josh called, picking the little dog up. The puppy stared at him, his gaze feeling like an accusation. "Not too much longer and you get to go, too."

"I didn't get an answer," Kerri advised, coming back. "No voice mail, either. I thought everyone had voice mail."

Josh put Rufus down on the floor and the little guy headed

back to the bedroom where the box lived. "He's wondering where his family is," Josh murmured. He knew what it was like, how loudly the silence of those empty rooms could ring upon the ears.

Suddenly Lucy's head whipped around. With a small whine, she clicked over to the window, her ears stiff.

"What is it, Lucy?" Kerri asked. Josh didn't tell her, but he knew what it was.

A Jeep stopped in the driveway next to Kerri's car and Lucy went to the door and scratched at the jamb, putting her nose to the crack at the bottom of the door and inhaling with a deep, shuddering sniff, whining and barking with little distressed-sounding yips. Josh went to the door and opened it and Lucy rocketed out and ran across the yard and virtually tackled the woman with long black hair who stood next to her car.

"Luce! Luce!" the woman shouted, tears in her eyes.

Lucy was crying, sobbing, her stomach to the ground, her tail thrashing, rolling on her back and then jumping to her feet, kissing the woman's face, so overjoyed it was manic in her, unrestrainable. "Lucy, my Lucy dog." Serena wept, falling to her knees and hugging her dog.

Kerri came up next to Josh on the front deck and stood with her hand to her mouth. "My God," she breathed.

Josh had never seen anything like it—Lucy's elation, her ecstasy, was the absolute embodiment of pure happiness.

"Why didn't you tell me?" Kerri asked.

Josh shrugged. "I didn't want you to think I was doing it for you. I'm doing it for Lucy."

Kerri was silent for a long moment. "It's what Lucy wants," she finally stated softly. Josh shrugged, shutting the front door behind them to keep the heat in the house. They walked down the steps together.

"Okay, okay, Luce," Serena protested, laughing. As she stood up, Lucy jumped up, trying to kiss her face. "Down, silly. Stay down now." Lucy tried to sit but her tail was wagging too hard. She licked Serena's hand as if it held bacon.

"Josh?" Serena asked.

"Yeah. This is Kerri from the animal shelter."

Serena had beautiful eyes and caramel skin. She swept her thick hair away from her face as she shook hands with Josh and Kerri.

"My flight was late. Of *course*. I drove straight here. I just, I can't thank you enough for taking care of my Lucy dog."

"Don't worry about it. I mean, if it hadn't been for Lucy, the puppies wouldn't have made it," Josh told her.

As he said her name, Lucy glanced over at him.

"Animal shelter," Serena repeated, looking at the clipboard in Kerri's hand. "Is there something I have to do to get my dog back?"

"Oh, no, no. It's pretty obvious it's your dog."

They all laughed and then, as the laughter died away an odd tension rose up between them. Josh knew what it was: Serena wanted to take Lucy and leave and Josh didn't want her to go.

"I suppose you want to get going," Kerri encouraged. She could read Serena's mind, too.

"Oh, yeah, I have my sister and her kids coming over for a welcome home party," Serena answered with a light laugh.

"Could I have a minute to talk to Lucy?" Josh asked.

No one thought it was at all strange. "Sure," Serena agreed.

Lucy, however, wouldn't leave Serena's side until Kerri got the idea to open the door to the Jeep. The dog happily bounded into the front seat, ready to go home with her person in the familiar car. Josh stood with the door open and put his arms around Lucy and she licked his ear.

"You are such a good dog, Lucy," he whispered. "You saved the puppies. You were a good mommy dog and they all are going to good homes because of you." Josh gazed into her deep brown eyes and she seemed to understand what he was saying. "I'm going to miss you so much. I love you, Lucy. Good-bye. You are a good, good dog." Josh stepped back, closing the door. Lucy held his eyes a long moment, and then shifted her gaze to Serena, who was still standing with Kerri. Josh took a long moment to compose himself before turning around, his lips pressed together in a trembling smile.

"Can I pay you for . . . ?" Serena asked.

"Oh, no. Please," Josh replied.

"Okay then. Thank you again. Merry Christmas."

"Merry Christmas. Good-bye," Kerri said.

"Wait," Josh said.

TWENTY

Kerri was watching Josh as if afraid of what he was going to say next. Josh turned to look at Lucy, watching them patiently from the front seat of the car, and then looked back to Serena.

"Yes?" Serena asked, sensing something.

"It's just that you said you travel sometimes, and I was thinking, maybe next time you go out of town, if you want, you could leave Lucy with me." Josh shrugged.

"Oh, *yeah*, of course," Serena exclaimed. "That would be great."

"Great," Kerri echoed, sounding relieved.

It took Serena a full minute to get Lucy to quit licking her and trying to climb into her lap, and then the Jeep backed up and turned around. Josh saw Lucy watching him from the car window and, as they headed down the driveway, Josh lifted his hand and waved. "Bye, Lucy," he whispered.

He turned to Kerri and she stepped forward and put her arms around him and her head on his chest. "You *are* the man I thought you were," she breathed, her voice muffled. "I am so, so glad."

They went into the house. "Rufus!" Josh called. He

clapped his hands, whistled, and shouted the puppy's name several times. Finally Rufus emerged from the back room, looking irritated at having been awakened. He came out to the living room, sniffing, glancing around.

"They're all gone, little guy. So sorry," Josh informed him softly.

Kerri was on the phone, checking her voice mail. She hung up and turned to Josh, an odd look in her eyes. "I have to go."

Josh's shoulders slumped. "What? Why? I was sort of hoping . . ." Josh raised his hands, palms up, not sure he should articulate what he had been hoping.

"We're supposed to be closed but someone just showed up at the shelter with a dog, and Madelyn has to go home."

"What? It's like, Christmas Eve eve, why didn't you just tell the people to come back later?"

"That's not what we do, Josh. It's fine."

"It's fine that people just dump their dogs? So the dog is just suddenly abandoned by his family? At Christmas?"

"No, of course not, that part's not fine. I mean it's fine that I go in to the shelter. Madelyn has kids; I don't. It's the holiday weekend."

"I'll go with you."

"Right, but you need to stay here for when the people show up for Rufus."

Josh glanced over at the sleeping puppy. "If they show up."

"Sure. I don't know what the story is on that." Kerri shrugged.

"You want to bring the new dog out here?"

"Maybe." Again, there was that odd expression in her eyes. What did that *mean*?

"So, I mean . . . Look, I was hoping . . . are you coming back?"

Kerri smiled at him. "Sure. Tomorrow, I'll be out."

"Tomorrow," Josh repeated, his voice full of disappointment.

"Let me give you my cell phone number," she told him. "So you can call me."

"Oh? You sure we're ready for that?"

She studied his face, then smiled. "He tells a joke," she proclaimed.

Rufus was unimpressed when Josh explained it might be the last time he would see Kerri, even when he picked up the snoozing puppy and held his tiny nose to Kerri's cheek. "The people will be out to pick you up, Rufus. Say good-bye."

"He looks mostly just sleepy." Kerri laughed.

"Sorry about that."

"No, it's fine. Really. Not every good-bye needs to be a big deal."

It felt to Josh as if Kerri were about to deliver another of her canned speeches, but she seemed to think better of it. She went outside and then, with a little wave from the front seat of her car, Kerri was gone.

"She keeps leaving," Josh told the puppy in his arms. "I have to figure out what to do differently so she'll want to stay here."

Josh was tense the rest of the day, waiting for the people to show up for Rufus. The sun, blocked by a mountain to the northwest, left the sky early, and night settled down around Josh's part of the hill without anyone pulling into his driveway.

"Just great," he muttered, irritated that he'd basically done nothing all afternoon but stress about something that didn't happen.

Rufus yawned and went to the door, so Josh let him out and he squatted in the yard, looking over his shoulder as if asking him to make note of the fact that he'd asked to be put outside to do his business. "I get it, you're a genius dog," Josh enthused.

Rufus sniffed at the grass a little, maybe smelling the scents of the rest of his family, and then trotted back over to Josh, who picked him up and carried him inside.

Josh heated up some macaroni and cheese and boiled a hot dog. Rufus slept on Lucy's pillow, not interested in Josh's culinary skills. After dinner, Josh settled down with a book, with Rufus lying on his chest. The little dog fell right to sleep.

Before he went to bed, Josh trooped out to his connectivity corner to send Kerri a text message with his cell phone:

I'm keeping Rufus.

She didn't reply, so he didn't know if she got it or not. He didn't call her to find out, though. He didn't want to talk about it.

If he'd used the PC to send the text, he would have had much more confidence that the message would go through without problems. He didn't bother to wonder why he'd decided to use the cell phone instead.

The next morning Josh took a hammer and began dismantling the puppy box. He carefully withdrew the nails so that he could burn the wood in the fireplace without accumulating a pile of metal in the ashes. The boards he stacked to carry to the woodpile, the blanket he decided to leave right where it was, so if Rufus needed the comfort of something familiar, it would be there for him. It's what Josh would want, anyway, if he were Rufus.

Just as he was finishing, he heard a very odd sound from the living room, a little noise that caused him to pause, cocking his head. He heard it again, and Josh grinned. Rufus was barking, pulling the sound out of the deepest part of his throat so that he sounded hilariously threatening.

"Okay, guard dog," he called.

Kerri must be here. Josh ducked into the bathroom and made sure his hair looked okay. He brushed his teeth and swigged some mouthwash. He smelled under his arms and decided he passed inspection in that category, though just to be safe he applied another layer of deodorant. Then he splashed a tiny amount of cologne on his neck, sniffed, and then wiped furiously at the smell on his neck with a wet washcloth.

All this time he expected to hear Kerri's steps on the front deck, and either her knock or the sound of the door opening, but he heard nothing.

Rufus gave another yip, abandoning the menacing tone and switching to an impatient, let-me-out-to-play bark.

"Hey, buddy, is it Kerri? Is Kerri here?" Josh asked, emerging from the bathroom. Rufus was at the big window, his little tail wagging stiffly. Josh walked up and stood behind the puppy to see what Rufus saw.

There were two cars parked side-by-side at the top of his driveway, and two people standing and talking to each other. Both were women. One of the women was Kerri.

The other one was Amanda.

Josh's heart felt as if it were beating sideways in his chest. He swallowed, not sure he trusted his eyes on this one. *Really?*

Amada's hair was different—she no longer had bangs, and it only just touched her shoulders instead of descending past them. Other than that she looked the same. Josh even recognized the sweater she was wearing as one he'd bought her, a black one, and the jacket was the ski vest he'd purchased for her when he took her skiing in Breckenridge the last time. Both Kerri and Amanda were smiling at each other and chatting and nodding, which seemed to Josh to be a completely unnatural state of affairs.

"I don't want to go out there, Rufus," Josh whispered faintly. The puppy didn't look at him—Rufus's attention was fixated on the two women. Sighing, Josh opened the front door, Rufus scrambling between his legs and bounding down the stairs in a half-falling puppy gait.

"Hi, Rufus!" Kerri called. Rufus went to Amanda first, though, smelling her outstretched hands.

"So *cute*," Amanda gushed. She straightened, tossing her head to sweep the hair out of her eyes, and smiled at Josh.

"Hey, stranger," Amanda greeted softly.

"Hi," Josh replied awkwardly.

Rufus ran to Kerri and started obsessively sniffing her boots, probably smelling all the dogs at the shelter. Kerri stooped and stroked Rufus but her eyes were steady on Josh.

With a little laugh, Amanda held out her arms and stepped up to him and Josh stiffly hugged her. She offered her cheek for a kiss, but as Josh moved in, she switched it up on him so that they were briefly mouth-to-mouth.

"We pulled in the driveway at the same time. I kept looking in my mirror, thinking, why is that car following me? Anyway. That is the cutest puppy," Amanda said. She lingered, holding Josh for a few seconds after his arms dropped.

"Cute puppy, what a concept," Josh replied. He felt a tremor pass through him, as if his body were under tremendous pressure, about to blow. Amanda's car, he noticed, was filled with boxes in the backseat, looking very much the same as it had when she'd moved out.

What did *that* mean?

But, of course, he knew what it meant. He'd already fantasized the scene countless times since that day last April when she'd left.

Josh felt seasick. He wanted to close his eyes and open them and be somewhere else.

Amanda was beautiful. Everyone said so, and everyone

was right. And wasn't it her whimsical and capricious desires that he loved most about her? She might always be dissatisfied with things, but wasn't that itchy wanderlust what had led them on so many fun adventures in their time together?

All this he processed as if someone were sending a text message directly into his brain. He gazed at Amanda with something akin to remorse filling his heart.

"Your friend was telling me about you fostering the puppies. That's so cool," Amanda praised, her smile flashing.

Josh cleared his throat.

"I wish I could have been here to see all of them," Amanda continued brightly. "You know how much I love dogs. Has fostering puppies changed your mind about getting one, Josh?" Amanda glanced over at Kerri. "I've wanted a dog, but so far he's been resisting me on it."

"Is that so," Kerri responded politely.

"Amanda," Josh interrupted, finding his voice.

She looked at him expectantly. Josh nodded at Kerri. "Kerri isn't a friend, exactly."

Both women watched him with unreadable expressions, waiting.

"Kerri is my girlfriend."

Amanda and Kerri looked equally shocked. "Oh," Amanda said finally.

Josh looked at Rufus, who was still sniffing Kerri's legs. Then he looked up at Kerri, who smiled. Josh smiled back.

"I'm sorry," Amanda apologized to Kerri, flustered.

Kerri waved her hand. "No problem."

Amanda nodded to the house. "So do you . . ."

"No, I'm not living here or anything," Kerri answered.

Yet, Josh wanted to say, but he didn't.

"I see." A brief calculation passed through Amanda's eyes, and if Josh hadn't known her so intimately, he probably would have missed it. But he spotted it and, when he glanced at Kerri, he knew that her ability to read minds was fully intact on this one as well.

"This is, well . . ." Amanda laughed, as if they all knew what she was going to say, and there was an extent to which Josh thought they probably did. "I'm sort of moving out. I did move out. Of the place in Fort Collins," she explained.

Josh looked at her. Amanda bit her lip, and then her eyes danced merrily at him, the way they used to when she would suggest on a Saturday afternoon that maybe they should go back to bed for a "nap." "Let an old friend sleep on your couch?" she asked him softly.

Josh could feel Kerri watching him. "Probably not a good idea," he responded.

Amanda looked wounded. "Josh, it's Christmas Eve, and I . . . I really don't have any other place to go."

"Oh," Josh replied. "Of course. What was I thinking?"

osh reached in his pocket for his wallet. "I've got two hundred," he stated, counting it out. "That should set you up for a night or two somewhere." He held the money out to Amanda, who was doing her wounded-look thing. There'd been a time when Josh would do anything to make that look go away.

"It's Christmas Eve," Amanda protested faintly.

"You know where I would go if I were you is the Brown Palace," Kerri suggested helpfully, naming one of the area's oldest hotels—and one located conveniently all the way down the hill in downtown Denver. "At Christmas the lobby is beautiful."

"I don't need *money*, Josh," Amanda said, almost but not quite keeping the anger from her voice. She pointedly didn't look at Kerri. "I wanted to see you."

"It was nice to see you, too, Amanda," Josh agreed.

She gave him a tight smile at his response, her eyes cold. Josh remained there and took it, knowing that she expected him to fold. The wind kicked up, rocking the trees with audible creaking sounds, and the three of them stood silently.

"I'd better get going," Amanda finally decided, her eyes on Josh.

"Merry Christmas," Kerri said happily.

Amanda turned and focused on opening her car door, pressing her lips together in a thin line. Josh scooped up Rufus and stood next to Kerri as the car started and drove off. He waved, but Amanda didn't.

When the sound of Amanda's car had completely faded away, Kerri turned to Josh, shaking her head. "I'll say this, with you it's never dull," she admired.

"You told me one time that nothing I'd ever done suggested any kind of thing between us," Josh explained. "I wanted to correct that."

She tossed her head at him. "So I'm your girlfriend now? Because it's sort of the first I've heard of it."

"Sorry if I was presumptuous," Josh apologized, not sounding sorry.

"That's okay. I liked it." They smiled at each other. "Sort of blew Amanda away, though," she observed.

"Oh, let's *not* talk about Amanda."

Kerri laughed.

"Come on," he suggested. "Let's go inside. I have a Christmas present for you and I can't wait until tomorrow."

"Me, too, but wait." Kerri went to the back of her car and lifted the hatch. She opened the sagging dog crate, reaching inside for a puppy.

It was Cody.

When she put the little dog on the ground, Rufus romped up and bowled right into him, the two of them rolling together in a hilarious tumbling jumble.

"Cody!" Josh called, slapping his knees. "Here, Cody!"

Cody and Rufus were far too involved with greeting each other to pay any attention to Josh. Kerri pulled a small package out of her car and stuffed it in her coat pocket and the four of them—two people and two dogs—went into the house. Cody followed where Rufus led him, only stumbling at the first and last steps on the wooden stairs to the front deck.

"Did you get my text?" Josh asked.

Frowning, Kerri pulled her phone out. "No, I didn't. When did you send it?"

"Last night. Probably it's in my phone and you'll get it next time I drive down the hill and back into cell range."

"I didn't get your call, either."

"Huh. Was I supposed to call?" He gave her a sideways glance.

"So what did your text say?"

"What happened?" Josh asked instead. "With Cody, I mean."

"Oh. That was the message I got last night. The family that adopted him was way out of their depth. They didn't realize what a huge difference it would make for a sightless dog to be blind from birth. The dog they had before was more than half a year old when she went blind, so she already knew the layout of the house, where the furniture was, and was already housebroken. Poor Cody has spent the last two weeks bumping into things and crying all the time. He couldn't find the puppy pads they put out for him, and he kept getting lost. I guess the whole family was one big nervous breakdown. They didn't even call, just showed up yesterday and handed him to Madelyn like they were re-turning a pair of shoes or something. I don't get people."

"So what happens now?"

Kerri blew out a puff of air. "So now we put him back on the website, I guess. He's so cute; we had a lot of inquiries about him. We just have to sort through them all and find the people who are able to take care of a blind dog."

"I guess no, that's not going to happen."

A smile played on Kerri's lips. "What do you mean?"

Josh nodded to where Rufus and Cody were playing on the floor. "This is as happy as Rufus has been since Cody left. I wouldn't think it was possible for a puppy to be de-pressed, but now that they're back together I see what was missing. Rufus needs Cody, and Cody needs Rufus."

"I thought it might be something like that."

"Far as I'm concerned, the people who were supposed to come yesterday lost their option when they didn't even bother to call. I don't care if they were kidnapped by aliens—they missed their opportunity."

"Right. You sure you're up to it, though? Two puppies, one of them blind?"

"Will I have help?"

"You mean from Rufus?"

"I mean human help."

Kerri grinned at him. "Do you *want* human help?"

"Yeah. I do. A *lot* of help."

"Right."

"Like, constantly."

"Understood."

Now they were both grinning. "So, hey, I want you to open your gift!" Josh exclaimed.

Underneath the tree was a big wrapped package, easily eight times the size of a bread box. "That's for me?"

"Yes."

"What is it, a new refrigerator?"

Josh laughed. "Just open it."

Kerri took off her coat, tossing it on the couch, and bent down to the gift. At the sound of ripping paper, the puppies stopped wrestling and bounded over to see what was going on, Rufus tight against Cody's left side.

"Hey!" Kerri shouted in delight. It was a new dog crate. "This is exactly what I need!"

"Oh, I know," Josh assured her.

The dogs were ripping up the paper, shaking it like they were killing snakes.

"Now this," Kerri said. She crossed to him on the couch, reached into her coat pocket, and pulled out a wrapped package, about the size of a hardback book.

Josh unwrapped it and opened the box. Inside were two leashes and two dog collars, each with a name tag on it. One said "Rufus," the other, "Cody."

"We make them right at the shelter," Kerri explained, "so this is more of a thought-that-counts gift than anything."

"So you knew I was keeping Rufus? I thought you didn't get my text."

"I knew because I didn't get your *call*. I figured there was only one reason you wouldn't want to talk to me, one thing you didn't want to tell me."

"It's like you can read my mind."

"Exactly."

"Well, stop that."

Kerri laughed.

"Seriously, have you always been psychic?"

"I'm seriously *not* psychic. I had no idea what was going on when this blond woman showed up, driving like ten yards in front of me all the way from downtown Evergreen to *your house*. And then when it turned out to be Amanda . . . I thought it was going to happen again."

"What? What was going to happen again?"

"That just when everything was looking like it was perfect, something would come along to wreck it."

"Yeah. For a second, I thought the same thing."

They smiled, holding each other's eyes.

"So let's not let anything wreck anything ever again," Josh suggested.

They stood in front of the Christmas tree and kissed while the dogs continued their deadly assault on the wrapping paper. There was something about the way she fit into his arms that felt more right than anything in the world.

"You know what I want to do?" Kerri said.

Josh involuntarily glanced down the hallway toward his bedroom and Kerri laughed, pushing at his shoulders. "Not *that*," she mock scolded.

"I asked you to stop reading my mind," Josh protested.

"I was thinking we could take the puppies and go downtown and just soak in the holiday, you know? The people will all be out, and carolers, and the lights—it's the best part about living in a small town, don't you think?"

It *was* the best part. There *were* carolers, and the stores were all beautifully lit, looking to Josh like a giant reproduction of the village on his mantel. The dogs were not at all sure they approved of the leashes at first, twisting and yanking at the unfamiliar sensation of being led, but after a time seemed to accept them. The two of them were close together, sniffing furiously at all the new scents.

At Evergreen Lake they stopped to watch the flow of skaters circling on the ice. Josh blinked when he saw Chuck, the brother of little Juliet, stream past on his skates. He turned his head and examined the benches lining the lake and saw the little girl first, and then the little puppy in her lap. He led Rufus and Cody over to see Lola.

"Lola!" Josh called. Juliet set the puppy down and the three siblings went crazy, jumping all over one another. Juliet giggled, her mittened hand to her mouth.

"I guess I never considered this could happen," Josh told Kerri while the puppies played.

"It will keep happening," Kerri replied. Josh searched her face. "You never even asked, but all of the people who adopted your puppies live right here in Evergreen. You can have playdates. That was part of the interview process."

"Wow," Josh said, contemplating.

Lola eventually decided she'd rather be held by Juliet, who scooped the little dog back up and held her like an infant. Josh waved good-bye to Matt, who was standing where he could keep an eye on both of his children, and Matt waved back.

Kerri and Josh walked on, and, when the snowflakes began drifting down, the people on the lake cheered and applauded.

"White Christmas," Josh murmured. He pulled Kerri in for a kiss and then just held her so that he could look into those blue eyes.

"You know what, Kerri? You're my Rufus," he told her.

She peered at him. "I'm your dog with a brown spot over my eye," she translated.

"I'm like Cody. I don't always see things, even things right in front of me. But you nudge me in the right direction. Like returning Lucy to Serena. Like letting go of the puppies. Like putting Amanda's pictures in a plastic box. You help me find my way in the world."

Her lips twitched into a small smile. "Is that the speech you give to all the girls?"

"Yeah, it's my standard." He nodded.

She grinned more broadly. "Pretty good."

He suggested they stop by the grocery store, where the deli just happened to have an order waiting for him—a fully cooked turkey dinner. "Traditional Christmas Eve food," he explained.

"Right," she approved. "But I thought you were an expert at turkey."

It was still snowing: huge flakes that flared in the parking lot lights. "Let's go home," Kerri suggested, the most welcome words Josh had ever heard.

The dogs seemed to really appreciate the smells in the car but were soon asleep in their new crate as they drove up the hill.

Josh put the turkey in the oven to keep it warm. He opened a bottle of wine and settled on the couch and Kerri came over and sat with him, leaning up against him. He put his arm around her. He'd never felt more comfortable. The dogs woke up and soon were back to wrestling on the floor in front of the fireplace.

He had to do something different, he'd told Rufus, to get her to stay.

"You know, Kerri," he said. She looked at him. "I keep trying to capture one last Christmas in this house that was like it used to be, and I've never managed it. But now, with you, it's like I want new Christmases. New memories. Nothing would make me happier than to wake up tomorrow morning and have you here with me. Could you maybe not go home tonight?"

"Hmm . . . ," she mused, which could be yes or could be no. "Sort of, what did you say? Presumptuous. Assuming I am ready to just stay here tonight, on the basis of what, you calling me your girlfriend? Like, that's all it takes?"

The fire crackled, drawing their attention for a bit. Josh shifted uncomfortably. What was he doing wrong?

"Right," she responded finally, "I guess you'll have to get my suitcase out of my car, then. I packed so much stuff this morning I could barely lift it."

He nodded carefully, afraid his grin was betraying the *yes!* echoing in his brain.

"So where would I sleep?" she asked after a moment.

"Oh. Sure. I mean, you could have the master."

"And what about you? Would you be in your old bedroom?"

"Of course."

She smiled at him and his heart started pounding. "Well, maybe not," she speculated.

"Okay."

They sat in a comfortable silence, her head on his shoulder, him holding her tight.

"You're the one, Kerri," he murmured, the words coming out unplanned. "The one I've been waiting for. The one I need."

She sighed in his embrace, moving even closer.

He couldn't explain it to himself, but somehow this woman in his arms had managed not to just save Christmas for Josh, but to save everything else, as well. She was his rescue. The life that had never made any sense to him at all now seemed to make all the sense in the world.

After a few minutes of just holding each other on the couch, Josh began to sing. Instantly the two little dogs at their feet stopped playing, whipping their heads around toward her.

Away in a dog box,
a quilt for their bed,
The little dog puppies
lay down their sweet heads.

The puppies both sat, paying rapt attention.

"Why aren't they falling asleep?" Kerri asked him.

"I don't know. Never failed before." Josh looked at her. "I love you, you know."

"I love you, too, Josh."

They smiled into each other's eyes. After a bit, Josh turned back to the puppies, who had resumed playing.

Lucy your mommy
Is gone for today
But she will come visit
So you guys can play
So sleep, little puppies
Together as one
And when you all wake up
We'll have puppy fun.

"You just make up those new lines?" Kerri asked.

"Yeah," Josh replied proudly.

"Sounds like it," she observed.

They laughed. The dogs still weren't sleeping, so Josh and Kerri moved on to "Silent Night," their voices joined together. And that's how they spent the evening: singing to the Dogs of Christmas.

Oliver

As they drove up to their house, Ed's dog was already at the Jeep's passenger side window, whining with urgent anticipation. Ed laughed softly as he shut off the engine and leaned across to let Oliver barrel out, turning his face away from Oliver's whipping tail. His dog had climbed into the car with this same eagerness, happy to be going wherever it was Ed was taking him, happy to get there, happy to leave. Oliver's sheer joy about everything was reinforced by the white markings on his brown muzzle, giving him a perpetual grin.

It was a short dash to Ed's front door, but Oliver managed to make it a one-dog stampede, going full tilt up the walk and miscalculating his launch onto the porch so that he slid face first into the door with a quiet thump.

"All right, buddy," Ed chuckled as he mounted the steps. He reached around to his backpack and jangled out some keys, letting Oliver sniff them before turning the lock and pushing into the foyer, Oliver pressing past him to chase old scents with a lowered nose and clicking nails. Ed took a breath of stale air. "Home," he pronounced, dumping his backpack. He left the heavy wooden door open, the screen door sighing shut behind him.

Oliver was storming up the stairs and racing around when Ed returned to the Jeep for the groceries, but the dog was soon yipping through the screen door, frantic that his person might go somewhere and leave him behind. Bags under an arm, Ed pulled open the door and reached down with a weathered hand to shove away the assault, struggling not to drop anything. "Oliver, you crazy mutt, I didn't go *anywhere*. Stop!"

Oliver tracked his person to the kitchen and then suddenly remembered his dog door, squeezing through to inspect the backyard at full gallop. Ed was folding the last bag when Oliver returned, looking somewhat puzzled that the yard and fence were exactly the same as they had been two months ago. Apparently, after so many weeks of new experiences around every bend in the trail, it was unfathomable to Oliver that some places just remained as is. "Find anything out there to chase?" Ed asked.

Oliver crossed the kitchen, went to the screen door, and sat, looking back over his shoulder with an expectant expression.

"We just got here and you're ready to leave again? You don't want to maybe sleep a few nights on a real bed?" Ed asked gently.

Oliver turned to the screen again, sniffing the world.

"We've got something very important to do this Saturday, Oliver. We're going to stick around for a few days, if that's okay with you."

Oliver didn't respond to his name. That night, though, he leapt nimbly up onto Ed's bed, turned in a couple circles, and lay down with a groan, as if the mattress were somehow less comfortable than the sleeping bag the two had shared the past two months.

Ed's hand draped lazily across Oliver's head, stroking silky ears and smoothing his brown fur. "You're a good, good dog, Oliver. I can't wait for Saturday. You are going to be so, so surprised."

Lola

Juliet had decided to face her Saturday wearing her Wonder Woman T-shirt and a pair of shorts with smiling frogs scattered across them. She was reading a book, which Lola had sniffed and found lacking, apparently unimpressed that it was at the fifth grade level even though Juliet had only recently graduated from third. The two of them were sprawled on the couch, Lola draping her thirty pound body across two pillows because the cushions alone were not soft enough. Lola's short, pointed ears twitched as she slept.

The girl stirred and Lola drowsily opened her eyes. The smell of Juliet, the sight of her, filled Lola with love. It was like warmth, this feeling.

"Daddy?"

Now Lola snapped awake, gazing at Juliet alertly. The girl's call had a note of expectation in it. *Car ride? Treat? Walk?*

"Daddy!" Louder this time.

"Yes honey?" That was the man who lived here, speaking from the other room. He was important to Juliet and therefore important to Lola. She called him "Daddy" and the woman named "Mommy" called the man "Matt."

"How much longer until we leave, Daddy?"

"We leave in about an hour."

Juliet kicked her legs. "An *hour*?"

Lola waited patiently to see if there was something going on that a dog should get involved with. Juliet sighed. "Lola, this is going to be so much *fun*," she whispered. She reached out a hand and Lola gave it a gentle lick, almost quivering with her absolute affection for this little girl.

Sophie

Andy led Sophie on a leash until they were through the second gate of the dog park, and then with a snap she was untethered—but not free. Her attention was locked on the tennis ball in Andy's hand, freezing her in place as securely as any physical restraint. He was smiling at her, waving the ball, her eyes tracking it every second.

"Just throw it," Jody suggested softly, coming to stand next to Andy.

Sophie's mouth dropped open and she tensed, her white-tipped tail completely rigid as Andy cranked his arm back. Then she was rocketing after the ball, so excited she over-ran it. She pounced, scooping it up, then turned to look back at her people.

Andy raised his hands to his mouth. "Bring it back!"

Sophie play-bowed, chewing the ball, pretending to drop it.

"Sophie!"

She knew if she waited that Andy would come to her. No one could resist such a wonderful toy, not for long. She wagged, waiting for Andy to give chase. He rolled his eyes at Jody.

The dog park was a vast enclosed space, fenced in all around, with a stunning view of the mountains, but Sophie didn't take in any of that. She was focused on the ball.

She knew there were other toys in the car. She had smelled them all the way here. If Andy brought out another one she would chase that one too, but she wasn't about to return any of them. The toys were *hers*.

When the gate opened moments later, Sophie carried the ball with her to greet the new canine, who loped into the fenced enclosure and ran straight at her on long, clumsy legs. The dogs pulled up short before they collided with each other, then reacted with shocked delight. Sophie knew this dog! This was her *brother*! They had been littermates before Sophie went to live with Andy and Jody and all of their wonderful dog toys.

Wagging so hard their tails shook their bodies, the dogs examined each other. Humans could do wonderful things but this new one, reuniting brother and sister, had the two canines absolutely amazed.

Sophie dropped the ball and then jumped on it, bowing and wagging, overjoyed to show Oliver her toy. He was not interested, which baffled Sophie—how could you not want a *ball*? He wanted to wrestle with her instead, and she had to relinquish the toy to engage him in play. The two of them careened around the park, shoulders banging into each other, exhilarated, jubilant.

Sophie did her best to steer Oliver back to where the ball lay nestled in the grass, but he seemed bent on pushing her into every corner of the dog park, stopping dead every so often to lift a leg, which she always examined politely. It was as if Oliver needed to explore every square inch of the place.

"We were hiking the Colorado Trail," Ed was saying to Andy and Jody. "Oliver carries one pack and I got the other. He loves the tent."

"If we did that with Sophie, we would need a separate tent just for her toys," Jody replied, glancing at her husband.

Andy shrugged. "I like to make her happy."

"She's happy now," Ed observed with a smile.

They turned as a truck crunched into the gravel parking lot. The doors opened and a man stood up out of one side and a little girl out of the other, followed by a brown and black dog who was smaller than Oliver and Sophie.

"I imagine that's probably Lola," Ed speculated.

Lola saw the dogs streaking across the grass over by the fence, but was clearly reluctant to leave Juliet's side until they were all through the double gates. Then Oliver came galloping at Lola while Sophie ran to grab her ball.

The little girl clapped her hands. "Lola! That's your brother and sister!"

Sophie realized with a certain amount of resignation that this new dog didn't know how to play with toys either.

She ran over to where Oliver was engaged with the female, overjoyed when she realized exactly who the new dog was.

What had recently become the most impossibly wonderful day had just gotten even better: this new dog was their sister!

Rufus

Josh pulled into a parking spot and stopped. "Looks like everybody else is already here," Kerri observed from the passenger seat.

"This is going to be fun," Josh replied. They grinned at each other. "Thanks for setting this up, Kerri."

Kerri twisted toward the back. Rufus and Cody were both sitting up alertly. Rufus was wagging because he could see dogs and Cody was wagging because Rufus was wagging. "You guys ready to meet your dog family?" Kerri asked.

Hearing a question in her voice and breathing in the scents of so many canines, the two dogs were nearly berserk with excitement, twisting their bodies into bounding circles as Josh exited and went back to lift the tailgate. As usual, Cody waited until Rufus had jumped to the ground and had turned around to wait. Rufus did not understand that Cody was blind, but he did understand that without him, his brother would be lost in the world. So Rufus was never far from Cody, always ready to turn him away from fences and other obstacles. He watched now as Cody sniffed, straining out beyond the bumper, locating Rufus's scent and confidently stepping into space, landing adroitly.

Rufus was wagging and agitated, wanting to charge in there and play with those other dogs in the park, but kept his pace steady and controlled as he guided his brother to the gate. Josh swung it open and Rufus sensed Cody getting ready to bolt forward, but there was a second gate so Rufus body-checked his brother. This was how it had always been, since they were tiny puppies, so Cody took the correction as a matter of course. Finally Josh opened the inner gate and Rufus ran straight toward the dog pack, careful to be within bumping distance of his brother so Cody would not lose his way.

Then they were in the middle of a joyous canine scrum. Rufus was astounded when his nose told him that he was with his siblings. His first family! The dogs heedlessly crashed into Cody, sniffing wildly, but Rufus could see Cody was not intimidated, so he allowed the chaotic scramble of dogs leaping and pawing each other to push his brother around.

After the sheer wonder of Sophie and Lola and Oliver and Cody and Rufus being reunited, the elated dogs turned as a pack and raced over to the humans who were standing by the fence. Josh and Kerri! For the dogs, having these two people there was cause for even more celebration. They jumped up, licking, loving, as the never-forgotten scent of their original people-family washed over them. They really went after Josh, nearly dragging him to the ground, Sophie and Lola crying out their delight.

"Okay, good, okay," Josh said, turning his face and sputtering as Sophie's tongue slathered his lips. "Enough, you crazy dogs! I love you too, now go play!"

It wasn't long before the whole pack was scrambling around the park's perimeter. Behind them Juliet tried to keep up, trailing a child's scent, a girl's giggle. Rufus could smell that the little girl pursuing them was the person who belonged to sister Sophie.

Rufus sprinted at full tilt, with Cody on one side and a sister on the other. It was the most joyous, joyous moment of Rufus's joyous, joyous life.

The People

"Your daughter is so cute," Jody told Juliet's father, Matt.

"Look at them go. I'm glad I decided this was worth coming back for," Ed said with a chuckle. "Appreciate you setting it up, Kerri. Don't know why we didn't do this sooner."

"Well, we figured if we didn't do it now, it would never happen," Kerri advised.

Ed cocked his head. "Oh?"

Kerri and Josh smiled at each other. Josh looked proud. "Kerri got into vet school at Michigan State. We're moving there next month."

"Congratulations, that's *wonderful*," Andy said heartily.

"So, you're moving there . . . permanently?" Jody asked.

Kerri shrugged. "Who knows. We'll decide what we want to do when I've graduated. Josh's job is virtual, he can work from anywhere, so we'll get out the map and see what appeals."

"Will you keep your place here, then?" Juliet's father wanted to know.

Josh shook his head. "Just listed it. We thought about renting it out, but my neighbor did that and wound up having to sue the guy staying there. Anyway, it's time to move on."

Kerri reached out and took Josh's hand.

"I was worried that the dogs wouldn't recognize each other," Andy confessed. "But look at them."

The people all smiled. The dogs were more than a hundred yards away, now, still moving together like a flock of birds. Juliet had stopped running and was watching with her hands on her hips.

Everyone was quiet for some time. "After my wife died," Ed finally murmured, "I didn't think I'd be happy again. But that crazy dog out there taught me that life's meant to be lived in the present. He's my whole world."

"Oh, I know it. Sophie and Andy go *everywhere* together. Mostly to PetSmart for toys, but everywhere," Jody replied.

"Sure," Andy said.

"That's like Lola and my little girl," Matt agreed. "The way that dog dotes on Juliet, I've never seen anything like it. Don't know what's going to happen when she's back in school in the fall; Lola even lies on the bathmat when Juliet's in the shower."

"It's the best thing, what you do," Andy told Kerri and Josh. "Finding lost dogs and putting them together with people? The house was so empty when my daughter left for college, I about lost my mind. But Sophie makes me happy."

"That's what dogs do. It's their purpose," Kerri said simply. "Making people happy."

Sophie grabbed the ball on the run and now she held it

in her jaws as the dogs chased each other around the park. She finally had what she wanted—her toy in her mouth, her siblings all pursuing her to take it away.

Lola had realized how far away they were from Juliet, so she broke away to dash back to the girl and the dogs all followed. The joy flowed between them like an all-embracing smell—every dog felt it, and every dog celebrated it.

They all turned, though, when they heard the unmistakable sound of the inner gate clanging shut.

Another dog had come to the park.

The New Dog

If this new arrival—a large brown and black canine with pointy ears—was intimidated by the pack thundering toward her, she showed no signs of it. She stood her ground as the siblings all bore down on her, as if confident these younger pups would break off their charge.

And that's exactly what happened. Oliver, in the lead, began to slow, and the others, bumping bodies, heeded the signal and faltered as well.

It was Cody, with his heightened sense of smell, who first realized who the new dog was, and he barked in celebration. Moments later, they all knew, surging up to the big canine, nosing her and play bowing and whimpering.

This was their mother dog.

They all wanted to jump on Lucy, but Lucy corrected them with a sharp growl they all obeyed immediately. She wanted to greet Josh, whimpering and licking, with the rest of the dogs plowing into him as if they were only now discovering he was there. He pushed through the milling pups, kneeling to take Lucy in his arms.

"How are you, Lucy dog? You good? I've really missed you," Josh murmured.

Lucy's person, Serena, bent down with a smile. "Remember Josh, Luce?"

Lucy would have been content to sit with Josh all day, but then he stood and slapped the dust off his pants. "Okay dogs! Go!"

They resumed running, Lucy in the lead, but their play was more restrained, because now they were following the alpha dog as she led them across the fields. Lola halted to sniff Juliet's outstretched hand before rejoining the pack.

When Josh used a hose to fill a large trough, the delicious smell of the water called to the dogs, sharp as a whistle. Panting, they lapped up huge gulps, splashing each other's faces in the process. Josh laughed at them.

Not long after that, the frantic pace of play slowed. Lucy found a place in the shade and collapsed, falling to her side. Each one of her puppies carefully picked their way to her, lining up as if they were back in the original den, falling on each other. Cody placed his head on Rufus's chest. Sophie had her ball within easy reach, ready to snatch it up if any of her siblings made a move. Lola and Oliver were in a sprawl, their heads pressed against Lucy's rib cage.

Lucy's eyes were soon half-lidded. She was happy to be living with Serena, her person, especially now that Serena no longer left on long trips. But she had never forgotten

Josh, and had never for a moment stopped thinking about her little puppies. Being back together with them was so natural, so right, and made her so happy.

Her eyes flitted open when she heard Serena laugh from the bench where the humans were all sitting, but when she closed them again, she slipped into a joyful dream, remembering licking her little blind puppies, feeling their tiny mouths as they fed, and nuzzling them, filled with love, as her litter slept at her side, just as they were doing now.

The reunited dogs dozed, content to lie together and remember when they were little puppies, dependent on their mother dog, piled together in a heap just like this.

Cody

"Lucy!"

Serena's call brought the canines to their feet as one. They shook themselves off and sniffed each other under their tails, bowing and yawning. When Lucy trotted to her person they all followed, Cody close enough to Rufus that their sides gently touched.

"Are you ready to go, Lucy? Say goodbye to your puppies."

Cody milled around with the rest of the dogs while people talked, and then the gates were opened and Rufus led him to out into a place of gravel and dust. Cody smelled his mother dog's scent abruptly fade when a car door slammed shut.

"Goodbye!" That was Lucy's person. Cody alertly tracked his mother dog as his nose and ears told him she was leaving.

When car sounds became distant, Cody's nose pointed in the direction Lucy had gone.

"This sure was fun," Ed remarked.

"When do you hit the trail again?" Josh asked. Hearing his voice, Cody turned his head toward Josh.

"Oh, probably not until August. These knees need a little downtime. Say goodbye, Oliver."

"We're leaving too. Thanks so much." That was Andy, one of Sophie's people. "Come on, Sophie."

Cody felt Sophie's nose touch him and turned, wagging, ready to play, but then Oliver and Sophie were gone, the car noises spiriting them away.

"Okay, Juliet, say bye-bye."

Small arms encircled Cody and he turned and licked the face that was in front of him. It was the girl whose scent had followed the dogs all day. "Bye, brother dog," she whispered. Cody wagged.

Soon Lola was gone. Cody turned for reassurance and Rufus was right there, solicitous, sensing that for a moment, Cody was lost.

"Time to go, dogs," Josh declared.

Cody heard his people leaving, Rufus trotting behind them, but for one of the only times in his life, Cody didn't obediently go where his brother led him. Instead, Cody turned his face back to the park, the heat from the grasses driving a faint current that brought with it the scents of the day. Cody smelled his sisters Lola and Sophie, his brothers Oliver and Rufus, and his mother dog, Lucy. Standing there, he remembered what it felt like to run with them, their bodies right there beside him as they all scampered around in endless, aimless circles. The scents led him to also recall their nap, when all the dogs were pressed together again, just as it had been when they were first born.

Rufus returned, nudging Cody expectantly. It was time for a car ride to some other place. Cody drank in one last, glorious scent from the dog reunion, and then turned to follow his brother.

It had been the most wonderful day of Cody's life, but tomorrow would probably be even better. It always was.

ACKNOWLEDGMENTS, EXPLANATIONS, AND APOLOGIES

This novel wouldn't even exist if not for Linda Quinton at Tor/Forge, who heard me describe a series of short stories I was thinking of writing about a man who winds up having to adopt out a bunch of puppies and exclaimed, "I want that as a book!" Thank you, Linda, for your vision and your trust.

My editor, Kristin Sevick, helped me find the right direction for *The Dogs of Christmas*—thanks for your ideas and suggestions. They were right on, Kristin.

Having Scott Miller on my side is like having an uncle who is Batman. You are the best agent ever, Scott.

My friend for so many years, Dr. Deb Mangelsdorf, went to veterinary college so that she could give me expert advice when I started writing dog books. She guided me through all the particulars concerning dog pregnancy, labor, and other things I've never done. Thanks for everything, Deb.

The world of animal rescue was entirely unknown to me until my daughter, Georgia Lee, introduced me to the notion that we can save animals who, through no fault of their own, are lost, abused, abandoned, or unloved. Thanks to Life Is Better Rescue, for the amazing work you're doing intervening in the lives of these poor unfortunate pets.

Chelsea, you never said a bad word about anyone. Not you either, Eloise.

I wouldn't have any sort of career at all if people didn't buy my books, and a lot of people who have done so have gone on to join the conversation on the A Dog's Purpose fan page on Facebook or to nominate their dogs for Dog of the Week on the adogspurpose.com website. I can't say it enough: Thank you for your support, and for loving the animals I write about.

And the team that helps keep it all going: Charlie, Chase, Trisha, Elliott. Thanks, guys.

Thanks to Leslie Rockiter, for cutting the book trailer, and to Dina Zaphiris, for training the actors in the book trailer.

Thanks to the geniuses at FlyHC.com for designing my websites and keeping them current. Come check them out at brucecameron.com and adogspurpose.com!

Thanks to all my friends at the Cypress Inn, for not letting people check in if they haven't read at least one of my books.

I speak for a lot of people and a lot of grateful animals when I say that there are so many wonderful people who use their position in the public eye to advance the cause of animal rescue and adoption. The originals were women like Tippi Hedren, Doris Day, Betty White, and Mary Tyler Moore—they showed the way. The new generation are people beautiful inside and out: Teri Austin, Elaine Hendrix, Ellen Laventhal, Katherine Heigl, and Elayne Boosler.

I want to acknowledge that the town of Evergreen does

exist, and that when I lived there you could go to the Evergreen Inn for great Mexican food. I want to apologize for any inaccuracies that have crept into my book regarding the town. I swear I heard Christmas carols playing from speakers mounted somewhere one December, but I couldn't find anyone who could verify this. And I'm sorry if I insulted your lake, but I'm from Michigan, guys, and there just seriously isn't enough water there to impress me. If you want, come up to Michigan sometime and make fun of our mountains.

Thanks to Moritz Borman, who has stubbornly refused to allow an injustice to stand. Thanks to my goddaughters, Carolina and Annie, for pretending I'm not too old to be talking to them, and to Steve for not getting any younger. Thanks to Hayes Michel, for being in my corner and assuring me that I'm not actually cornered.

Thank you to the cast and crew of the new film *Muffin Top,* for asking me to produce their movie and thus giving me a year's worth of distraction. Thanks especially to Mitzi Druss and Lydia Fantini, for doing such a good job on my hair and makeup that Cathryn cut my scene from the movie. June, you did an amazing job on my wardrobe— everyone *totally* bought the idea that I was an old white guy. I'd write your last name but I can't. Thanks to Tina Young, for traveling across the country to be in my scene. Thanks to Tom Rooker, for keeping an eye on my old house.

It may not take a village, but it takes a family. Thanks to my parents, Bill and Monsie, for never giving up and always supporting me, even when my back was repeatedly flat on the mat. Thanks to my sisters, Julie and Amy, for making sure everyone they know owns at least one copy of each one of my books.

And I really should thank my dog, Tucker, who gave me inspiration for this tale by living it. He was literally dropped off at birth in a cardboard box, and was left there overnight with his newborn siblings until someone found the box at the rescue shelter the next morning. Luckily my daughter was fostering a German Shepherd who had just weaned her pups, so Tucker was placed with a new mom, who accepted him and his siblings without question—probably just thought she'd had a wild weekend.

Finally, to the person who reads my early drafts and always helps me improve my work: Cathryn, you're the partner every writer dreams of. And now that I've married you, I get all the help for free!